Quincy's Quest

Martin Quincy finds himself unwittingly involved in a murder, following which he is beaten and left for dead in the Painted Desert.

On the run for a crime he did not commit, and valiantly responsible for an orphaned child, he must summon all his strength and determination to wreak revenge on the men who betrayed him and complete his most audacious quest yet.

By the same author

Saloon Justice

Quincy's Quest

Jay Clanton

A Black Horse Western

ROBERT HALE · LONDON

ISBN 978-0-7198-1573-7

Robert Hale Limited
Clerkenwell House
Clerkenwell Green
London EC1R 0HT

www.halebooks.com

Typeset by
Derek Doyle & Associates, Shaw Heath
Printed and bound in Great Britain by
CPI Antony Rowe, Chippenham and Eastbourne

CHAPTER 1

They say a man can go three weeks without food; but only three days without water. Still, as the Good Book says, 'Man shall not live by bread alone' and there are other things which can sustain a body, besides food and water. The thirst for revenge, for example.

It was now a shade under three days since so much as a drop of water had moistened the parched and cracked lips of Martin Quincy; but still he was alive and his body was functioning well enough to keep him moving across the barren landscape. True, he was in a lamentable state, but Quincy's fierce and unquenchable lust for vengeance against the men who had left him helpless and alone in the desert, prevented him from lying down and dying. He was damned if he would die before settling accounts with them.

Quincy had picked up with the three men when they invited him to join a poker game in a cramped and poky cantina on the road to Maricopa Wells. He

5

had been down on his luck and drifting slowly south towards Tucson in the hope of finding work. He had a little stake money, just over twenty dollars, and managed to hold his own in the game; ending about ten dollars up by the end of the evening's play. Several times during the course of the game, Quincy had looked up to see one or other of the men staring at him speculatively and in the end, he had said irritably, 'What are you fellows looking at, so? Do I have a smudge on my nose or something of the kind?'

'Don't take on,' said the man who called himself Ryan, 'We've been looking for a body to help us in a little work. You look a likely enough type. How about it, you want in?'

'The hell kind of a question's that?' asked Quincy. 'In on what? What is this work?'

'Not here,' said Ryan softly, 'Let's you and me take a little walk, down the road a ways.'

The three men were so obviously up to no good, that Quincy thought at first that they might be planning to rob him. Well, that was fine, if they wanted to try it. Nobody had yet succeeded in the whole course of his life in taking advantage of Martin Quincy in that way. He got to his feet and as Ryan also stood, said to him quietly, 'Just the two of us, hey?'

'Surely,' said the other man, looking a little puzzled. Then he twigged and said with a laugh, 'Ah, you don't trust us, is that it? Think we're going to jump you for your money? Nothing o' the sort.'

Once they were walking side by side in the darkness,

Ryan said, 'Would you call yourself an honest man?'

'What is this, you a priest or something? What does it matter to you how honest I am?'

'Here's how the land lies. Me and my friends have it in mind to undertake a little business with the Southern Pacific Railroad Company. We need another pair o' hands. It's not such as would suit a fellow who is too much worried about honesty and suchlike. So if you're a delicate type, best tell me now and we'll forget the whole thing.'

'You mean a robbery? How much we talkin' of here?'

'If you're in, then your share'll be better than three thousand dollars.'

'How long'll this "work" take?' asked Quincy.

'No more than half an hour.'

Beggars can't be choosers and the way things had been going lately, it wouldn't be long before Quincy was indeed next door to being a beggar, so he had agreed to join in with whatever project it was that Ryan and his two friends were involved in. This turned out to be holding up and robbing the *Tucson Flyer*, as it approached Maricopa Wells on its way to Yuma. There would be, according to Ryan, over $12,000 in gold coins, contained in a safe in the express car at the back of the train.

At various points in his life, Quincy had stolen cash money. The money had always belonged to large companies; he would have scorned to steal from an ordinary man like himself. He didn't like such activities much, but needs must when the devil drives. None of his previous thefts had entailed coming face to face with a man and stealing from him directly; they had been frauds and cheats, rather than straightforward robberies. Nevertheless, times were getting harder and harder, and Quincy had a hankering to give up his wandering life and put down roots somewhere. Maybe a little farm or something of that sort. He wasn't eligible under the Homesteader's Act to a quarter section, having had the misfortune to have fought on the losing side in the war, so he would need to buy such a place for his own self, using money which he had raised. Three thousand dollars might just do the trick. It was this dream of his which blinded him to the fact that holding up a train was a horse of a very different colour from most of the schemes in which he had been mixed up over the years.

According to Ryan, the *Tucson Flyer* had to slow down to a crawl as it came nigh to Maricopa Wells. Ryan and his friends would tackle the express car, but they needed a man to hold the driver and stoker at gunpoint and ensure that the men didn't try to start moving the train until the robbery had been successfully concluded. The railroad line ran right along the edge of the Gila Desert and they would make their escape in that direction; losing any pursuers in the trackless wastes of that bleak and inhospitable wilderness. After riding into the desert for a day or two, they would then emerge miles from the scene of the robbery and go their own separate ways. And all this would earn Quincy just over

$3,000, which would, God willing, be enough to set him up in a little place of his own.

When a man is coming up towards forty years of age, as Quincy was in that year of 1882, he sometimes finds that he wishes to slow down a little and settle somewhere quiet for a spell. Somehow, Quincy had never managed to save any of the money that he made since the war; it had run through his fingers like water. The prospect of having a substantial sum of money now, an amount which would set him up comfortably somewhere, was an all too attractive one to a man who only had a little over thirty dollars to show for his whole life's work to date.

So six days after that poker game, Martin Quincy found himself mounted on his horse, with his neckerchief pulled up over his mouth and nose, waiting by the side of the railroad about five miles from Maricopa Wells. The *Tucson Flyer* was due in no more than a half hour and his role in the affair was simply to haul himself into the driver's cab and then order the driver at gunpoint to bring the locomotive to a halt.

The initial stages of the robbery went as smoothly as you could hope. The train toiled up the steep incline leading to Maricopa at no more than a brisk walking pace. Perhaps the driver had seen the four riders up ahead, but if so, there was little enough that he could do about it. The locomotive was working flat-out, just to haul the line of carriages up the slope, so there was no question of speeding up.

When the train was just fifty yards from them,

Quincy dismounted and ran towards it. He grabbed a hold of the rail alongside the cab and then pulled himself up. Neither the driver nor the stoker seemed to be unduly surprised at this development. They had probably guessed what was in the wind, as soon as they had caught sight of the four men waiting for them. Quincy pulled his pistol and, without actually pointing it at either of the other men, said, 'You know what's needful. Just do it now and we'll be off and away in next to no time.'

The driver was an old fellow of about sixty. He looked at Quincy with undisguised contempt and said, 'You're like to hang for this, if anybody gets hurt.'

'Nobody's goin' to get hurt. Not if you all do as I say now.'

The driver applied the brakes and with a great hissing of steam and screeching of steel on steel, the train ground to a halt.

Quincy didn't see anything of the actual robbery, his part in the business being limited to ensuring that the train itself remained stationery during the proceedings. He found it a mite embarrassing to stand there in that small compartment, pointing a gun at the two men. After a few seconds, he tried to relieve the tension by saying, 'Have you fellows been working long for the Southern Pacific?' They both ignored him and he did not speak again.

Perhaps two minutes after the train had been stopped, there came the sound of a pistol shot, away at the other end of the train, where the express car was located. There was no more shooting though and Quincy's mind was eased when he realized that there was not going to be some kind of gun battle. No more than five minutes later, Ryan and the other two rode up and demanded to know whether Quincy wished to accompany them or if he would prefer to stay there and wait for the law to catch up with him. He swung down, and then mounted his horse. The four of them then cantered off into the desert.

'Say,' said Quincy, 'What happened back there? I heard a shot.'

'What do you care?' said one of the others, a man called Tucker. 'We got the gold, which is all that matters.'

Thinking back on it later, Quincy knew that this was the point at which he was aware that things hadn't gone well. At the time though, he was so anxious to put as many miles between himself and the Southern Pacific Railroad Line, that he did not pursue the matter further and just kept on riding.

That evening, they divided up the spoils. The safe had contained exactly twelve thousand, eight hundred dollars; all of it in gold. According to Ryan, this money was bound for the banks in Yuma. Each of the four men accordingly had three thousand, two hundred dollars in ten dollar gold pieces. Quincy had never seen so much money in his life. He reached into the saddle-bag where he had placed his own share and ran his fingers through it, hardly able to come to terms with his good fortune. On an impulse, he took out a handful of coins and thrust them into the pocket of his pants.

Their ride had taken them deep into the Gila Desert, and Quincy knew that he would have been hard pressed to find his own way out of the rocky wastes. If it hadn't been for that, he most probably would have left the other men and been on his way immediately. As it was, he felt that it would be madness to leave their company until they were at least clear of the desert. He calculated that they were probably the better part of thirty miles now from the edge of the arid wilderness.

The fourth member of the band, a short, foul-mouthed Mexican called Lopez, was telling a dirty story and since this was not the kind of thing which Quincy cared to hear, he went off, away from the others, on the pretext of making water. He walked a fair distance; there was no danger of becoming separated from the three other men, because he could hear their voices, laughing and shouting profanities. When he returned, he found that the other men were talking about the recent hold-up of the train. It was a moonless night and they had not yet seen him, so Quincy stood stock still and listened; wondering if he would find out what that shot had been about.

'He was one stubborn bastard, him in the express car,' said Ryan, whose voice was distinctive, 'I don't think he believed we'd do it.'

Lopez said, 'He learn different, no? His face when you shot the woman! And then when you offered to kill her child as well, that got results.'

The others laughed, but then stopped when Quincy walked into their midst. He said, 'Hey, don't let me spoil your fun. What's this about shooting a woman?'

'Let it go, Quincy,' said Ryan easily, 'We got the money, that's all that counts.'

'What happened to the woman?' asked Quincy again, this time with a noticeable edge to his voice. 'I got a right to know. If we're caught, then I'll get the same as you men. What happened?'

'Ah, that's nothing to the purpose,' said Tucker, 'We ain't agoin' to get caught, so it doesn't matter.'

'It matters to me,' Quincy said sharply, 'I'm asking you straight Ryan, what's this about shootin' a woman?'

'Well if you'll have it, then here's what chanced when we went to get the express car opened up. It was armoured, with a stout door which only had a little slit in it, covered with wire mesh. The guard, he peers out and says, "I ain't lettin' you boys rob this car and there's an end of it!" So I sent Lopez here, off to fetch a woman. The one he picked had a child with her, little boy, eight or nine and he insisted on coming too.'

Tough as he was and despite being a veteran of the Civil War, Quincy felt the blood draining from his cheeks as he listened to Ryan's account. He said, very quietly, 'Please tell me that you didn't kill her?'

'We ask the man to open up the car,' said Lopez, 'But he say, "Get to hell, you bandits!" Then he say, "You wouldn't kill an innocent person. You bluffing." '

13

Ryan said, 'So I shot her then and there. Right through the head. Then I said that if he wouldn't open up the door, I was going to kill the child next. Then he let us in, opened the safe for us and we were done. There, are you happy now?'

'What sort of men are you?' asked Quincy, wonderingly. 'I never heard the like.' He turned away, hardly able to speak with amazement and shock. It was at this point that one of the other men, he had no idea which, had leaped nimbly to his feet and swung a rifle butt into the back of Quincy's head. He was vaguely aware of falling and the others crowding round to pummel and kick him. Then there was blackness.

When Quincy came round it was still night, although the moon was a good deal lower in the sky than it had been. He figured that he might have been out for four or five hours. His head hurt most of all, but he was covered in aches and bruises pretty well all over, as far as he could make out. For a few seconds, he just laid there, trying to work out why Ryan, Tucker and Lopez had attacked him so viciously. Had they always intended to treat him so and deprive him of his own share of the proceeds of the robbery? Or had they perhaps been angered and dismayed by his reaction to hearing of the woman's death? Did they fear that he would turn state's evidence and hand them in to the law? Whatever the explanation, thought Quincy grimly, they would have done better to have killed him rather than just rough him up like this. He turned over and the pain in his head increased dramatically.

As he had more than half expected, the others had gone, taking with them his horse, along with his share of the gold. Quincy got unsteadily to his feet, intent upon finding what the other three men *had* left. The answer to this question was short and sweet. They had left him nothing at all. Not a canteen of water, nor morsel of food. Then he realized that his gun-belt was also missing. Those cow's sons had left him helpless and unarmed in the middle of the desert.

It did not take long for Martin Quincy to run through his choices. They boiled down essentially to either lying down right there and waiting for an agonizing death from dehydration or trying to save his life by finding a way out of the desert. Having summed up the case so succinctly, it seemed to him absurd to tamely accept death. The only question now was which way to walk.

The first thing to do, before even thinking about moving, was to orient himself and figure out which way was north. Quincy found the group of seven stars known as the Gourd and followed a line through two of them, which pointed to the Pole Star. He calculated that this direction would lead straight back to the edge of the desert where he and the other three men had entered it. That was no good, though; the last thing he wanted to do was walk right back to where the robbery and murder had been committed. He accordingly turned a little to his left and plotted a course north-west. How far had they ridden yesterday? Thirty, perhaps thirty-five miles? It was impossible to say with any accuracy.

The other major consideration was when to do his walking. It made no sense to make the journey during the day. He would be dead from water loss by sunset. The only sensible dodge was to walk at night and then sleep during the hottest part of the day.

So began the longest, and by far and away the worst, three days of Martin Quincy's life. He started walking as soon as he had worked the case through in his mind. The sooner he began this journey, the sooner he might find water. The first night was bad, because he felt sick and in great pain from the beating he had received. Somehow though, he kept going, always making sure that he was heading just a little to the left of the Pole Star. What a mercy, he thought, that the sky was mostly clear in the desert. Without the stars to guide him, he would have been altogether lost.

When the dawn came, Quincy kept going until the sun began to feel warm on his back. Then he looked around for some shade where he could shelter during the hottest part of the day. He settled on a large boulder and tried to make himself comfortable by leaning against it. For several hours, he dozed fitfully; not really awake and yet unable to sleep properly. When the sun had passed its zenith and was sinking towards the western horizon, he set off again, attempting to follow the same course as he had been the night before.

Another night came and Quincy kept trudging

north-west. The Gila Desert seemed to stretch for infinity; every part of it exactly the same. The boulder he rested by on the second day was so precisely similar to the one in whose lee he had dozed twenty-four hours earlier, that he began to think that perhaps it *was* the same boulder and he was going round in circles. By the third night, Quincy was delirious and hardly able to set one foot in front of the other.

Had it not been for that fierce desire to be revenged upon the men who had abandoned him and left him to die, then Martin Quincy would just have sat down and waited for death to overtake him. It was only the thought of those three men which kept him going. He muttered over and over again to himself as he stumbled along, 'I won't die. I won't die.' Yet at the back of his mind was the belief that he probably would die, alone out here in this cursed desert.

The end came with shocking abruptness. The swollen red globe of the sun was just grazing the horizon as it sank, when Quincy realized that he was no longer walking across bare grit. Instead, there were scrubby plants beneath his feet. In another few hours, it would be dark and he would have been walking for three whole days. As if in a dream, he was aware that the thistles and withered grass had given way to cultivated land; tall, spindly stalks of corn. He heard a strange creaking noise, which was tantalisingly familiar. Suddenly, he knew what it was. A wind-pump was turning nearby, the blades of its wheel revolving in the evening breeze. He stopped walking and looked about him properly for the first time.

He had reached some farm buildings. There was a tumbledown wooden barn and a few low sheds. Near the metal tower of the wind-pump was a horse trough. Quincy staggered towards this and plunged his head and shoulders into the water. He knew that it would be fatal for him to gulp down as much water as he wished at once. His belly would swell up and he would, at the very least, be sick. He forced himself instead to take frequent, small sips. The water in the horse trough was stagnant and green, but never had any drink tasted sweeter to the desperate man. He knew now that he was going to live after all.

CHAPTER 2

'You want that I should put a little pomade on your hair?' asked the barber, after he had finished his ministrations.

Quincy looked at himself in the mirror. He saw a very different figure from the gaunt-looking scarecrow who had practically collapsed on the edge of town a week ago. 'No, I reckon I'll do well enough without any o' your grease,' he said pleasantly. 'What do I owe you?'

It is amazing the difference that a haircut and shave can make to a man's appearance. Quincy had suffered no lasting ill effects from his little sojourn in the Gila Desert; a touch of sunburn and a severe case of dehydration, nothing that a couple of days' rest wasn't able to put right. What a mercy that he had thought to plunge his hands into that three thousand dollars' worth of gold coins which had briefly been his. He found when he counted that he had pulled out twenty two of them and thrust them in his pants on an impulse. Those skunks he had rode with might have taken his horse, his gun and his share of the gold, but they hadn't thought to go through his pockets. He was accordingly pretty well placed from a financial point of view; at least for the next few weeks.

Having had that vision of a little place to call his own, a small farm where he could settle down and live quietly, Quincy was loathe to see it snatched away so suddenly by that trio of villains. He had a crow to pluck with them anyway, for leaving him for dead in the middle of the desert, but more than that, they had his share of the plunder from the robbery of the railroad train. His present train of thought entailed killing the three men who had treated him so and recovering at the very least, his own share of the booty.

'Well, sir,' said the barber, 'I should say that you look a different man.'

'I reckon you're just about right there, my friend,' said Quincy cheerfully, as he paid the man, including a generous tip.

The unimaginatively named town of Gila's Edge was the very epitome of the one-horse town of which folk sometimes talked. There was a barber's shop, general store, church, blacksmith's forge, tiny saloon and that really was about it. Quincy was renting a room over the saloon and had picked up all the gossip that was current in Gila's Edge while drinking at the bar. It didn't amount to much. News of the hold-up of the *Tucson Flyer* had certainly not reached the town, nor had any of the three men

Quincy was seeking.

Having bought a horse the previous day, a sturdy little Indian pony that would do just fine for rough travelling across the country, the only thing that Quincy now lacked was a pistol. The general store had a faded and weather-worn painted sign by the door, which proclaimed 'Tinware & Guns'. He hadn't seen any pistols on display when last he had been in the store, but maybe the owner kept them out back or something. He surely hoped so, because the idea of tracking down those men without a gun at his hip was not an enticing one. His luck was in, though.

'A gun, sir?' said the storekeeper, 'Why, yes indeed. We ain't got what you might call a great selection, but we have a few, sir. Let me step out back a moment and fetch them through.'

Old Mr Carter, who ran the store, had been speaking no more than the literal truth when he said that he didn't have a great selection. Indeed, he was understating the case. There were only three guns to choose from and two of them were the same model: two Remington 1875 Army 0.44s and an old Cap-and-Ball Navy Colt. 'Jeez,' said Quincy, 'This all you got?'

'That's it. Folk round here don't have much call for going heeled. It's a quiet little place, you might have noticed.'

One thing was for sure, Quincy had no intention of carting around some weapon that would need reloading from a flask of powder. He set the Navy

Colt to one side and picked up one of the Remingtons. 'You got cartridges for this?'

'Sure. I'll fetch you out a box.'

While Mr Carter was fussing around in his back room, Quincy tried the trigger action on the Remington. It seemed smooth enough, but when he spun the cylinder, he could see at once that there was a definite bias. He picked up the other pistol and tried that. It seemed a better bet, with no notice-able faults. The old storekeeper set down the box of ammunition and Quincy reached over and opened it, extracting a couple of shells. 'Hey, you ain't about to load that thing in here, I hope?' said Mr Carter nervously. Quincy laughed.

'You can rest easy. I just want to check the date on these things.' Quincy held one of the brass car-tridges up close, so that he could read the year stamped on the rim. It was '79. 'You got any newer than this?' he inquired.

'No, sir, that's all there is.'

'Well, I guess I'll take this pistol and this box of cartridges.'

Having paid for the items, Martin Quincy went out into the street and sat down on the boardwalk. He loaded the pistol and then stood up and tucked it into his belt. He felt all the better for being armed again. Inevitably, old Mr Carter had charged him a good deal more than the gun would have cost in a big town. When a man stumbles into your town, more dead than alive and lacking the necessaries of life, it is only human nature that you should try and gouge him as hard as you can for anything he needs. Quincy would have done the self-same thing himself and he didn't hold any grudge about it. Everybody in Gila's Edge whom he'd come into contact with so far had cheated and exploited him, and he would be glad to shake the dust of that place from his feet, which he purposed to do later that same day.

The only question now perplexing Quincy was the direction in which he should set out. When he got back to the tiny room he was renting over the saloon, a little cubby hole about the size of a broom closet, he laid down on the bed and reasoned the matter through.

The men he had been riding with had made no special provision for a lengthy journey through the desert, which would seem to rule out their heading south towards the Mexican border. They would hardly head back towards Maricopa Wells, nor for the matter of that, towards Tucson. They would run the risk of encountering a posse in that direction. They hadn't left the desert here at this town, which almost certainly meant that they had passed to the west of Gila's Edge. All the signs, as far as Quincy could calculate, suggested that Yuma would be their destination. He decided to have a little siesta before setting off later that afternoon. He lay back on the bed and closed his eyes. Before falling asleep, he muttered out loud, 'I'm coming for you bastards, just you wait and see. I'll kill every one of you.'

Beating Quincy half to death and then abandoning

him helpless in the desert had been Jethro Ryan's idea. To give him his due, Ryan hadn't originally intended to behave so towards the new member of their group. It had been Quincy's shocked and disgusted reaction when he heard about the murder of the woman which had sealed his fate. As soon as Quincy had turned away in horror, Ryan knew that it would not be safe to let this fellow walk away. Being a man who acted immediately on his impulses, which was both his great strength and also his besetting weakness, Ryan had leapt to his feet and swung the butt of his rifle as hard as he could into the back of the other man's head. At his urging, Lopez and Tucker had then helped him to administer a thorough and scientific beating. At the last moment, Ryan had baulked at shooting the unconscious man in the back of the head, so they had contented themselves with robbing Quincy of all that he had and leaving him there to die.

After roughing up Quincy, the three bandits had headed north-west, towards Yuma. They had reached that bustling town after five days and only killed one person on the way there. This inquisitive individual had, in a sense, brought about his own death.

Twelve thousand dollars in ten dollar gold pieces weighs a considerable amount. Each coin only weighs half an ounce or so, but when there are 1,200 of them, that works out at a little over thirty seven pounds in weight. Ryan, Tucker and Lopez had divided the coins into three equal portions and packed their bags with them. Tucker, who was neither the brightest nor the best-organized robber to be found in Arizona, had brought along a worn and frayed old carpet bag to carry his share of the money after the raid on the railroad train. People generally just put clothes and suchlike in carpet bags, and encountering one which weighs better than twelve and a half pounds and consequently feels like it might be full of lead, is such a novelty that it was bound to excite curiosity at some point.

A couple of days after they left the desert, the three of them fetched up at the town of Endurance, which lay on the railroad line between Yuma and Maricopa Wells. Here, they decided to book into a hotel and rest up for a while. They chose the smartest place in town; an imposing, white stucco building not far from the railroad depot, called The Metropolitan. After all, money was no object.

'What in the hell is a metropolitan?' asked Jack Tucker.

'Is a mystery to me,' admitted Lopez. 'What do you say, Ryan? Are you knowing what this metropolitan is meaning?'

'No, I don't. What d'you boys take me for, a walking dictionary? Let's just get our gear stowed here.' Ryan jumped down from his horse and unfastened the leather saddle-bag containing both his clothes, shaving tackle and $4,000 in gold.

The Metropolitan was such a swanky joint, that they employed uniformed pageboys to meet patrons at the door and see to the stabling of their horses round the back, if need be. These youths also vied with one another to carry folk's bags up to their rooms, this being a surefire way of earning a tip. Jack Tucker, who was taken aback by the attentions of these young fellows, yielded up his carpet bag to the foremost boy, saying, 'You take a care of that now.'

Billy Squires, who although only fifteen years old, was as sharp as you like, knew at once that there must be something interesting in that bag. It weighed a ton; it surely had a deal more inside it than just a couple of shirts. Ryan growled at the young fellow who tried to carry his bag and Lopez aimed a cuff at the nearest of the boys, indicating that they would do better to keep clear of him. So it was that although all three of the men suffered their horses to be led round the back of the hotel to the stables, only Tucker's bag was handled by the staff at the hotel.

The boy kept tight hold of Tucker's bag until he had been registered and given a room number and key. Then Billy trotted along up the stairs behind Tucker, and carried the bag into his room and placed it carefully on the bed. Tucker handed the boy a dime and thought no more about it. A half hour later, he and his two companions were dining in the bar-room and washing down their food with draughts of beer to wash the dust of the trail out of their throats.

Of all the pageboys at The Metropolitan, none was sneakier or had a greater eye to the main chance than Billy Squires. He was always snooping in people's rooms when they were out, trying to see who was well-off, which customers might want an introduction to a prostitute, who the gamblers were and many other things. His wage was not a high one, and it was by getting tips for various services over and above his duties at the hotel, that young Billy managed to make ends meet.

As soon as he was sure that the man whose bag he had carried was safely occupied with his vittles, Billy borrowed the master key and went up the back service stairs to the second floor of the hotel. He slipped into the man's room, closing the door behind him quickly. He knew very well that if he was caught entering a room in this way, the least he could expect was to be discharged without a character. He could even end up being arrested on suspicion of theft. Still and all, he just had to know what Mr J. Tucker was toting in that old carpet bag of his.

The bag wasn't on the bed, nor under it either. Billy eventually found it in a drawer in the bureau, and eagerly undid the clasp and peered in. To his utter amazement, he found that it was filled with gold coins and in an instant, he knew just what this was all about.

Although the towns in this corner of Arizona were a little isolated and newspapers were not a common sight, folk living in them nevertheless managed to hear much of what was going on. The telegraph line running along the side of the railroad was one source; another was the passengers and crew of the trains which stopped over in Endurance to take on water and fuel. One way and another, they were up to date with major events in the territory. Word of the ambush and robbery of the *Tucson Flyer* had come humming down the wires a matter of hours after it had taken place.

His hands trembling a little, Billy Squires fastened the clasp on the carpet bag and carefully closed the drawer. Then he left the room at once and went back to the stairs, where he sat down to reason matters out. He had not the slightest doubt that the man in room 14, he who called himself Tucker, was one of those who had held up the railroad train a day or two back. The question was, how could he make the most capital out of that knowledge? Blackmail the owner of the carpet bag? Turn him in and seek a reward? Steal the gold for his own self? Billy's mind was in a whirl and he knew that if he sat here much longer, his absence would be noticed. He accordingly made his way back down to the ground floor, where he began clearing away glasses from the tables in the bar.

Tucker was sitting at a table with the two men he had arrived with. Like as not, thought Billy to himself, they were also involved in the robbery and perhaps had bags of gold themselves, hid away in their rooms. The thought of all that wealth made the boy feel a little giddy.

'Don't look round sudden, now,' said Ryan to the others, 'But take a look at that lad over yonder, on the other side of the room.'

Lopez and Tucker both yawned and stretched artistically, glancing in the direction that Ryan had suggested. 'What of him?' asked Tucker. 'He's just picking up glasses from all that I am able to collect.'

'He's been staring sideways at the three of us, from the moment he come in here,' declared Ryan, 'Mark what I say now, he knows something.'

Lopez laughed easily and said, 'Ah, you worry a whole heap, my friend. Half the time about nothing.'

Ryan ignored the Mexican and said to Tucker, 'Is that the boy who carried your bag in here?'

Tucker took a quick look and said, 'They all look the same in those damned costumes. Could be, I guess. What of it?'

'Have you got shit for brains or what?' inquired Ryan solicitously. 'He like as not felt the weight of your bag and then went up to the room and looked around since we been sitting here.'

There was a deathly silence, as the other men digested this theory, which, now that it had been spelled out for them, sounded all too plausible.

'What should we do, d'you reckon?' asked Tucker, who always took his lead from Ryan.

'There's only one thing to do,' said Ryan, 'You ain't neither of you got squeamish, I hope?'

Lopez smiled broadly. 'We draw straws to see who does it?'

'No,' said Ryan, 'I'll do it myself. I don't trust you two not to screw it up.'

As evening was falling, Billy still hadn't been able

to make up his mind the best way to take advantage of the knowledge that he had acquired. He knew that he would have to act fairly quickly and would have been glad of some advice, but at the same time he was loathe to share the information about the train robbers. Thinking about all this made him a little careless; the boss yelled at him and reminded Billy that there were plenty of other boys in town who would be glad to step right into his job if he thought that he wasn't up to it any more. This was alarming, so the young man began working briskly and shelved the problem of what to do about the gold until he finished work at around nine that night.

At about quarter to nine, one of the men who had arrived at the hotel with Mr Tucker caught Billy's eye and called him over to where he was sitting alone at the bar. 'I think you and me might be able to undertake a little business, young fellow,' said this man in a low voice.

'I don't rightly understand you, sir.'

'Well now, it's easy enough. There's $500 for you, waiting right this minute. All you need to earn it is to keep your mouth closed. That make it any clearer?'

This was a dream come true for Billy. Here was how he could make a pile of money from his discovery and he hadn't even needed to try and put the bite of the men; they had come crawling to him. 'Well now, I'll have to think it over . . .' began Billy.

The man smiled and said, 'I wouldn't exert yourself in that direction, son. I'm making you a right good offer. What time do you finish up here?'

'Maybe another five minutes.'

'Why don't I meet you round the back, by the stable in, say ten minutes? You ain't told anybody else about anything, I suppose?'

The boy grinned at that. 'No, sir, I ain't as stupid as I look!'

Ten minutes later, Billy Squires was waiting anxiously in the alleyway at back of the hotel. This was the biggest break he had had since starting work at The Metropolitan, six months ago. Five hundred dollars! Of course, he had every intention of turning those men in after he had cashed in himself. He'd no idea what sort of reward was being offered for those who had robbed the *Tucson Flyer*, but he had no doubt that it would be a substantial one. The clock above the railroad station struck the hour and Billy looked round to see if the man who had arranged to meet him had turned up yet.

Out of the darkness came a soft voice. 'You there, son?'

'Yes, sir, I'm standing right here,' replied Billy and these were destined to be the last words he ever spoke in the whole course of his life.

Ryan, Tucker and Lopez checked out of the hotel the next morning and carried on towards Yuma. It was another two days before somebody working in the stable uncovered young Billy Squires, where he had been buried in the muck-heap at the end of the yard. It looked as though he had been knifed. It was a dreadful business, but folk knew what a sly little devil he had been and it was guessed that his poking and prying might have angered the wrong person. Nobody thought to connect his death with the three men who had stayed the night at The Metropolitan.

CHAPTER 3

Augustus Birrell knew that the men who had robbed the *Tucson Flyer* of $12,000 were right there in Yuma. How he knew, he couldn't have said, and he certainly had no objective evidence for his belief. Nevertheless, he knew that it was so. When you've spent twenty years working for the Chicago Police Department and another five as head of security for a big company like the Southern Pacific Railroad, you get a feel for such things. There was no especial reason why the men should have headed for Yuma, rather than making a run across the border into Mexico, but Birrell was absolutely sure in his own mind that they were right here in town; maybe only a few yards from him as this very moment. He glared suspiciously at the nearest pedestrians.

Until a year or two before the war, Yuma had been no more than a railroad junction. There had been a water tower, stores of coal and a telegraph office and that was about all. Now, it was a sprawling town containing several thousand inhabitants. And it was still growing rapidly. Everywhere you went, you could hear the sound of hammering and sawing as more and more buildings were being thrown up. Rumour was that if things carried on like this, Yuma would be applying for a city charter in a year or two.

In such a bustling town, with men coming and going by the hundred, it might have seemed an impossible task to track down the four men that Birrell was hunting for. After all, he had only the vaguest descriptions and no real reason anyway for thinking that they were even in Yuma at all. You don't rise to the top of a city police force though, without learning a trick or two.

The Southern Pacific were plumb desperate to solve the crime that had brought them such bad publicity. Already, Wells-Fargo were capitalizing on the robbery and using it to promote their own secure network of coaches for transporting money from one city to another. Their proud boast was that there had never yet been a successful robbery of a Wells-Fargo security coach. It wasn't hard to see why. They employed ex-soldiers and police officers, paying them top wages and arming them to the teeth. No bandit in his senses would take on those men. Far easier to strike the express cars tacked on to the end of railroad trains.

Almost as bad for the railroad company had been the death of one of its passengers. There had been a dip in the numbers of those travelling the Southern Pacific since the *Tucson Flyer* had been hit, and it was vital to show anybody else tempted to prey upon the line that such crimes didn't pay. That was why Birrell was under enormous pressure from his bosses to catch the men responsible, and see them brought to trial and speedily hanged. It might act to discourage any others planning to undertake similar ventures.

It had taken Augustus Birrell ten days to work his way from Tucson to Yuma, via Maricopa Wells and various other towns. All the time, his bosses had been wiring him frantically, demanding to know what the Sam Hill he was up to and why he hadn't yet run down those scoundrels to earth. Mindful of the old fable about the tortoise and the hare, Birrell ignored all such exhortations and continued to plough his patient and lonely furrow. He had finally reached Yuma twelve hours earlier, and this morning, he proposed to begin in earnest his search for the men who he knew in his waters were hiding out here.

Birrell's first port of call that morning was a dingy little pawnshop in an alleyway off Main Street. It was run by a fellow called Feeney and the former detective had picked up some information about this man while he had been heading towards Yuma.

The bell tinkled cheerfully when Birrell opened the door to Abe Feeney's store. The owner came out to greet him. 'Good morning, sir. How may I help you?'

'I'm looking for some friends of mine. Three white men and a Mexican.'

Feeney chuckled. 'Well, I wish I could help you, but I buy and sell goods. I'm not an introduction agency.'

'Oh, that's a right shame,' said Birrell, looking crestfallen, 'I was hoping you could set me on the right path.'

A peculiarity of Augustus Birrell's, and one which marked him apart from most other police officers and inquiry agents, was that he never raised his voice, blustered or cursed. This was sometimes apt, as in the present case, to lead those with whom he had dealings to underestimate him and cause them to believe that they could jerk him around with impunity. Abe Feeney was one of those who fell into this fatal error. All he saw standing front of him was a mild-looking man in a collar and tie, with a derby on his head. He looked for all the world like a commercial traveller.

Birrell made as though to turn regretfully away. As he did so, his hand shot out and grabbed Abe Feeney's lower lip. He wrenched this sensitive body part with sufficient force to tear the soft membranes which linked the unfortunate store keeper's lip to his jaw. Then Birrell brought his hand down to the counter, compelling the injured man to lower his head, in order to ease the excruciating pain from his mouth.

In a shoulder holster under his jacket, Birrell kept a .44 Colt, whose barrel he had sawn off short, so that it would fit more comfortably under his arm. This meant that the weapon wasn't much use for long distance shooting, although it was fine for close-up work. It could hardly have been closer to Feeney, for the detective had drawn it and shoved it right in the groaning man's face. Then he said softly, 'I'm going to ask you one more time, Feeney. Three white men, travelling in the company of a Mexican. Bring anybody to mind?'

'Jesus, are you crazy?' gasped the man in agony. 'You ripped open my mouth, what's wrong with you?'

For answer, Birrell cocked the Colt. It was enough and Abe Feeney whimpered in fear. 'All right, I'll tell you what I know. Let me up though.'

Blood filled the storekeeper's mouth and some trickled down his chin on to his shirt-front. He reached down for a cloth and then froze when Birrell said, 'Make another move and you're a dead man.'

'I only want to mop my mouth!' said Feeney indistinctly through a mouthful of spittle and blood.

'Well, you reach down nice and slow, if you're looking for a rag or some such,' said Birrell, 'Mind, I've taken first pull on this trigger.'

After gingerly dabbing at his lip and spitting into the cloth, Feeney said, 'I think I might know who you're after. Friend o' mine changed some money for a man a few days back. Said only one man came in the shop, but there was a greaser and another white fellow waiting for him outside the store.'

'Changed money? How's that?'

'Fellow had a hundred ten dollar gold pieces. He wanted them changed for bills. My friend, he gave him eight hundred dollars in fives and tens for the hundred ten dollar bits.'

37

'So making himself two hundred dollars for five minutes work,' said Birrell thoughtfully, 'Why didn't this man go to a bank and get the full thousand for his gold?'

Feeney shrugged. 'How should I know? Maybe he didn't want to answer any questions about how he'd come by a load of gold ten dollar pieces.'

'Ah, yes. You think that him and his friends want to throw money around a little, but don't want to keep paying with ten dollar coins? Yes, it could be so. Where can I find this "friend" of yours?'

'Say, is this about that robbery, the train up by Maricopa Wells? Isn't there a reward for information leading to them responsible?'

'You want a reward, Feeney?' asked the detective pleasantly. 'Here now, I'll tell you what I'll do. You're a pimp, a shylock and you fence stolen property. You help me now to the very best of your ability and I won't go straight down to the sheriff's office and have you thrown into gaol. That a good enough reward for you? Where can I find your friend?'

At about the same time that Augustus Birrell was menacing the store keeper, Quincy rode into Yuma after a fairly gruelling journey. His main concern was to find a little rooming house where he could put up for a few nights. Before doing that though, he had promised himself a good long drink of ale. Leaving his horse at the hitching rail outside, Quincy entered the Girl of the Period and ordered a glass of porter. He took it over to a table, upon which a newspaper was lying. It was a copy of the *Tucson Weekly Intelligencer and Agricultural Gazette.* It was dated four days earlier and had presumably been left in the saloon by some passing traveller from the east. Quincy read the piece, which took up almost the whole of the front page.

HORRIBLE MURDER OF
RAILROAD PASSENGER
THE *TUCSON FLYER* ROBBED OF $12,000

On Tuesday last, a singular and atrocious crime of unparalleled ferocity was carried out against our territory's most famous railroad train – the *Tucson Flyer*. Four masked desperados halted the locomotive as it toiled up the incline to Maricopa Wells and forced it to stop, so that they might plunder the express car. The guard in the strong room, Mr DAVID CARSON, at first refused entry to the robbers and told them to do their worst. Tragic to relate, their worst was worse than anybody, including the hapless Mr CARSON, could possibly have envisaged. One of the villains was dispatched to the passenger coaches and returned with Mrs ESTHER HANIGAN and her eight year-old son GEOFFREY. Mrs HANIGAN is a widow, well-known in Tucson as being the gentlest of souls. She was reported to be travelling to Maricopa Wells to visit her sister. This innocent lady was promptly shot dead by the bandits, who then offered to kill her little son as well if further resistance was shown. Mr CARSON did the only sensible thing – opening the express car and allowing the thieves to help themselves. One of the men beat Mr CARSON round the head with a pistol, for not opening up immediately. The four men eventually made off with no less than $12,000, which was earmarked for the banks in Yuma. Mrs HANIGAN'S little boy is now staying with his aunt in Maricopa Wells. However, she is not a wealthy woman and the rumour is current that young GEOFFREY might have to be sent to the Orphans' Asylum in Tucson. We are reliably informed that one of Chicago's smartest detectives, Mr AUGUSTUS BIRRELL is on the trail of the malefactors. Readers will recall that MR BIRRELL was appointed Head of Security at the Southern Pacific Railroad Company and if anybody is able to bring the crime home to its perpetrators, Mr BIRRELL is the man for the job.

When he finished reading this article, Quincy stood up, went outside and was copiously sick, vomiting over the boardwalk, much to the disgust of passersby, who assumed him to be intoxicated. It was something far deeper than mere drunkenness that afflicted Martin Quincy, though. For the first time in fifteen years or so, he was racked with guilt; a guilt so severe that it had made him feel physically ill.

Since the end of the war, Quincy had made money

in practically any way which presented itself. He had run a bar, organized poker games, panned for gold, worked as a lawman and a dozen other things. His two or three forays into outright theft had been trifling affairs in which he had contrived to cheat banks or big companies out of their money. A couple of these schemes worked, one or two did not. He had never taken part in a robbery before, leastways not until a fortnight or so previously, and he had known very well when he agreed to team up with Ryan and the other two, that he was doing wrong.

Maybe it was seeing the names of the parties involved in the business, but until reading that newspaper, Martin Quincy had been able to view the murdered woman and her orphaned child as mere ciphers; abstract entities with no real and independent existence. Sure, he had been disgusted when Ryan and the others had told him about the murder of the female passenger, but even then he had managed to keep the death in a separate compartment of his mind; the lumber-room where he stuffed all those uncomfortable memories of things he had been involved in that he would sooner forget. Learning that the mother had been called Esther Hanigan and her son, Geoffrey, had shattered the comforting fiction. These were real, living and breathing human people who had nothing to do with him. Leastways, Esther Hanigan had been living and breathing until he had agreed to help with that damned robbery. And now her child, just eight years of age was like to end up in an orphans' asylum!

Quincy went back into the bar-room and ordered another glass of ale to rid his mouth of the bitter taste of bile which he had thrown up. He wanted to drink himself unconscious, to blot out the memory of that whole business and in particular the thought of that wretched little boy, motherless and heading for the orphanage. He tried to persuade himself that it was not really his fault. After all, he hadn't pulled the trigger and had he been present outside that express car, he would most certainly have prevented the murder. This didn't answer though; Quincy knew fine well that he had been part of the enterprise and shared the blame for what had chanced. The question was, what should he do now?

Handing himself into the law wouldn't help that poor little boy. 'Less seeing a man hanged who was partly responsible for his mother's death would be a comfort to the child. Quincy knew, with a sinking feeling, that he would never rest easy in his bed at night if he didn't try to do something for Geoffrey Hanigan. He could think later about settling accounts with Ryan and the others, for now he had to think of something practical that he could do to make any sort of amends to the boy he had so cruelly wronged.

Stabbing the troublesome youth in Endurance hadn't caused Jethro Ryan to lose so much as a second's sleep. The boy might have been young, but Ryan knew the type well enough. He was a black-mailer and even had he been paid off, he'd still've informed against them for the sake of a reward. The only safe thing to do with such creatures was silence them for good and all.

Apart from the stabbing to death of a fifteen-year-old boy, their journey to Yuma had been pretty uneventful. Now, the three of them were relaxing in an eating house. After they had had their fill and were drinking coffee, Ryan said, 'Well, you fellows, I guess this is where we part company.'

Lopez watched him with narrowed eyes, but Tucker looked aghast. 'Part company? Why, what d'you mean?' he said. 'We been together for the longest time. Why we goin' to split up now?'

'What's the matter?' said Ryan roughly. 'You not got enough money? You can do what you please. We've each got enough to settle down for a spell and take life quietly. What about you, Lopez?'

'Me?' said the Mexican, 'I am not ready to go home yet awhiles. Is true that this money will make me almost rich in my own country, but how dull! I want some more living yet, before I go to live on a little farm,' he laughed.

'Come to that,' said Tucker, 'I don't know as I want to retire yet awhile, myself. I'd sooner live it up a bit. You know, girls, cards and suchlike.'

Ryan looked thoughtful. He didn't speak for a while and then he said, 'So the two of you are saying as you want to carry on as we are? You don't want that we should stop now while we're ahead of the game?'

'Hell, no!' exclaimed Tucker. 'Let's keep goin'.'

The fact was that none of the three men at that table carried on in the way that they did wholly for the money. There was the excitement of the thing, the thrill of evading capture, the delicious feeling when a job was successfully pulled off. They were like opium users; hopelessly addicted to danger and risk-taking. Ryan had just wanted to see if the other two still felt the same way and so had offered them the chance to back out if that was what they wanted. He was right glad though that neither Tucker nor Lopez seemed inclined to stop at this point.

'Well then, boys,' said Ryan, 'What say that we find a game of good, high stakes poker tonight and maybe treat ourselves to a night at the cathouse? I hear there's a real dandy one here in town. Then tomorrow, I'll let you know what I got in mind. I think you'll like it.'

The others nodded and smiled. They were relieved that their leader wasn't really thinking of throwing in his hand yet awhiles.

Pete Owen knew bad news when he encountered it and the dapper little man standing at the bar in Pete's tavern had bad news written all over him. There was nothing outwardly alarming about the fellow; he wasn't even heeled that Pete could see. Just stood there at the bar, sipping a glass of whiskey. There was something almost feminine about the delicacy with which the man took little tastes of the amber liquid in the glass. Not that he was a soft one; far from it. Pete just couldn't make him out at all and that was troublesome in itself, because Pete Owen prided himself upon being a good judge of men. He needed to be, his livelihood, indeed his very life, depended upon it.

The bar that he ran was really just a sideline for Owen. He ran a lot of the rackets in Yuma, having a hand in everything from gambling and money-lending to prostitution and the supply of morphine. The bar that he operated was never busy, and most of those who called in for a drink were also doing business of one sort or another with the man behind the counter. It provided a perfect cover for Owen when some criminal was tailed to his saloon. He could say innocently to the sheriff, 'It's a tavern, what do I know about the folk who drop by for a drink? You want that I should check up on their life histories before I serve them a beer?' The law in Yuma had many suspicions about Pete Owen, but nothing had ever been proved.

There were only two other customers standing at the bar when Birrell walked in off the street. He didn't think that Feeney would have dared to give him the run-around, so Birrell was quite sure that the man serving him his glass of whiskey had actually seen with his own two eyes the men who'd held up the *Tucson Flyer*.

'Mr Owen,' said Birrell politely, after he had sipped his drink for a few minutes, 'I've an idea that you and me can do each other a favour.'

Owen started at hearing his name used by this stranger. He didn't exactly keep his identity a secret, but on the other hand, there was nothing in the gloomy little bar-room nor on the sign outside, to indicate what his given name might be. Whoever this unknown man was, he had obviously gone out of his way to make inquiries before fetching up here.

'A favour?' exclaimed Owen, willfully misunderstanding the situation. 'I can't be granting credit to you, if that's what you're hinting at.'

Birrell eyed the other man with amusement. 'Why don't you close up for the day and then you and me can have a little chat?' he suggested.

'Close up? What, you mean close this place? I'm sorry, mister, you'd have to be givin' me a damned good reason to do that.'

The words were no sooner out of Pete Owen's mouth, when the meek-looking soul at the bar produced a pistol from somewhere inside his jacket and commenced shooting at the bottles lined up on a shelf above the barkeep. Shards and splinters of broken glass showered on to Owen's head, combined with the contents of the bottles. The other two men standing at the bar bolted at once for the door. After firing three shots, which filled the room with acrid smoke, Birrell cocked the Colt once more and pointed it straight at Owen's face, saying, 'I'll warrant that you have a sawn-off scattergun under the counter there, just for such occasions as this. You want to see if you can reach it, before I shoot you down like the mangy dog that you are?'

'I reckon I'll pass on that,' said Pete Owen imperturbably, 'You said you wanted me to close up, I think, so as we could have a chat?'

'Yes, just lock that street door, only be sure to move as slow as you like. I'm a nervous kind o' fellow and when I get jumpy, I tend to shoot the first man I see.'

Owen was one of the toughest and most brutal, unprincipled rogues in Yuma, but he felt a shiver of fear as he watched the smartly-dressed man with the gun in his hand. He had not the slightest doubt that this fellow would kill him without the least hesitation if he didn't do just precisely as he was bid.

CHAPTER 4

As soon as they had hit Yuma, Ryan had shaved $200 each from Lopez and Tucker's share of the loot. He told them that the fellow who provided him with the information about the shipment of gold had agreed to settle for five per cent of the total haul. Since this man seemed to know all about the business and was probably aware to within a nickel how much they had taken, it would be pointless trying to chisel him out of his cut.

'There's another thing,' said Ryan to the others, 'Those banks as didn't get the cash that we lifted from that train, they're right edgy now. There's the fear that there might be what is known as a "run" on the banks, if they don't restock themselves with money soon.'

'So?' said Tucker. 'What's it to us if some big bank goes bust?'

Lopez said nothing, but watched Ryan with his sharp little eyes. He knew that there was something here to their advantage, or Ryan would never have bothered to mention the possibility of a run on the banks.

'You're a slow-witted son of a bitch, Tucker, you know that?' said Ryan irritably. 'I couldn't give a good goddamn about the banks going bust. You shut up and listen, I'll tell you how this works to our benefit.'

Tucker was used to being spoken to like this by the leader of their outfit and so said nothing more, but just listened carefully.

'So far, the banks have been paying out all right, but they're tryin' to delay handing out money when possible. Word's got around about that, which is makin' folk a mite worried. They all, meaning the banks, have got together to bring in a whole heap of cash from Phoenix. Now here's the good bit. They ain't usin' Wells-Fargo or nothing like that. They just chartered an old Concorde and are piling sacks of bills into it. It's comin' here soon and there'll only be a couple o' boys riding shotgun on it. It's ours for the takin'.'

'You say so?' said Lopez, his brilliant white teeth shining against his swarthy face. 'This is good, no? When is it due, this stage?'

'My man doesn't know yet. Soon as he does, he's going to tell me.'

Tucker and Lopez were very pleased to hear about the coach that they could rob. Since hitting Yuma, they had thrown a lot of money around and although they hadn't spent more than a couple of hundred each so far, it wasn't hard to foresee that if

they didn't replenish their supplies, then the two of
them would simply gamble away their substance at
faro tables and poker games.

Tucker had been playing roulette, a game with
which he was unfamiliar and not being too hot at cal-
culating odds, he had lost heavily the previous night.
His method was a simple one. He bet a dollar on
either red or black and then if that lost, he doubled
up his stake on the same colour at the next spin of
the wheels. Increasing your bets in a geometric pro-
gression like this is ruinous in the long run, as
Tucker had found out to his cost.

The problem with those boys was that while they
could get by on next to nothing when the circumstances demanded it, as soon as they did have money
in their pockets and were in a town, the whole
amount went rapidly on whores, rounds of drinks in
bar-rooms and gambling. That there was an opportunity to top up their cash reserves was welcome
news.

Quincy had come to a decision about his course of
action, at least for the next week or two. He hoped
that he could accomplish his plans without shedding
blood, but if that was necessary, then so be it. He
proposed to track down and recover his share of the
proceeds of the robbery and then take it over to
Maricopa Wells and see that Geoffrey Hanigan's
aunt received it, so that she could continue to care
for her late sister's child.

He didn't want to have to fight and kill for it, but

Martin Quincy was quite determined to have the $3,000 that he had earned during that raid. If Ryan and the others would hand it over to him peaceably, then he might even be prepared to foreswear his vengeance against them; much as he itched to shoot the three men who had betrayed him. But the needs of that poor little boy, who was like to be heading towards an orphans' asylum if Quincy did nothing, were paramount.

Of course, Quincy didn't know where Ryan, Tucker and Lopez might be found. He didn't even know for sure that they were even in Yuma. All he could really do was roam the streets restlessly, keeping his wits about him and his eyes wide open. For quite apart from his own plans, he knew fine well that if any of those three men saw him, then they would at once conclude that he had come seeking their blood and they would, in all probability, shoot him down before he had a chance to explain his real intentions.

Martin Quincy was not the only man in Yuma who was walking the streets all day, looking for the men who had robbed the Tucson Flyer. Pete Owen knew that from the man working for the Southern Pacific Railroad Company; he had met his match in ruthlessness and cunning. After his bar had been shot up, he had tried to bribe Birrell to forget all about him and leave him alone. That wouldn't answer and so he had finally admitted that he'd bought a hundred gold ten dollar pieces from a stranger, and paid him $800 for them.

'Where are those coins now?' asked Birrell.

'I passed them on to a contact of mine. They'll be halfway to California by now.'

The railroad detective looked long and hard at Owen, saying finally, 'You know that's compounding a felony? You'd have good reason to suppose that gold to be stolen property.'

Owen shrugged. 'It was a business deal. I didn't ask where the coins come from, he didn't tell me.'

'You'd know him again, this fellow?'

'Maybe, maybe not.'

'Don't you dare try to fox with me, Owen,' said the detective. 'For two pins, I'd turn you over to the law in Tucson for this. I tell you now, anybody connected with that crime in any capacity is like to draw a good long sentence, the way feelings are running there about the murder. How'd that suit you?'

'All right, happen I might recognize the man again, if I met him.'

'What about the others?'

'Others?' said Owen, in apparent perplexity, 'What others?'

'You're getting smart again. I know that you saw two white men and a Mexican. What, you weren't going to mention them to me? Didn't think I knew?'

'Oh, them!'

'Yes, them. Just cut the crap, Owen, and straighten with me. Talking to you's like dealing with a corkscrew.'

'They waited outside. I saw 'em through the window. Didn't get as good a view of 'em as the fellow who came into the bar.'

Augustus Birrell didn't see any percentage in letting it show, least of all to the scoundrel sitting in front of him, but he was highly satisfied with all this. There was no point in wringing a description out of Owen. It would be the same, vague word picture as had already appeared in the newspapers and across wanted bills all along the railroad line. But he had here a man who could actually identify at least one of the men, having seen him in person. He said to Pete Owen, 'You'll have to shut up shop for a few days, my friend.'

'Hey, what's that? I can't do that. Everybody knows where to find me in my bar. I can't just close up. You must be crazy. Why, I'd lose a fortune in business!'

'Yes, crooked business. Well now, the choice is yours. You can walk around for a day or two until we see one of those men you had dealings with or I can set out to make your life a burden. I'm right good at that, you take my word for it. You'll not only be driven out of business here, I'll see you in handcuffs and on a train to Tucson at the end of it. Which'll you have?'

When all was said and done, it wasn't really much of a choice. That bastard had him by the balls and he didn't strike Owen as the bluffing type. If he said he'd make Pete Owen's life a burden, then that was just exactly what he would do.

So it was that quite unknown to Ryan, Tucker or Lopez, three men were walking the streets of Yuma all day long, hoping to catch the merest glimpse of them. Despite the number of people now living in the town and notwithstanding the crowds arriving and leaving each day, it was only a matter of time before one of those looking for the three men should come across them purely by happenstance.

It was Quincy who first caught sight of one of the men who had left him for dead in the Gila Desert. He was walking along near the depot, keeping his eyes peeled, when he saw Tucker come out of a store. Swiftly, Quincy averted his face, so that the other man wouldn't see who was passing by. He sneaked a look out of the corner of his eye and saw that Tucker was ambling slowly back towards Main Street. Well, he had been right. The men he was looking for were in Yuma. At least, one of them was. Quincy had formed the distinct impression that Tucker was not the brightest specimen to be found, and most likely depended upon others to set up the crimes in which he participated. He would almost certainly not be operating alone here. If Quincy could only stick on his tail like a burr, then Tucker would probably lead him to the other two.

Following Tucker wasn't an easy job. The fellow looked to be as nervy as a cat. He was constantly glancing behind him and unexpectedly changing direction; darting down alley-ways and ducking into stores. He was clearly afraid of being followed. Quincy wondered if the law was on to the three men, but the actual explanation was simpler than that. When the three bandits had first hit Yuma, they'd booked into the very first hotel they had come across. It had proved comfortable enough, but Ryan had now found that an even better place had sprung up since he had last been in this town. It was better than The Metropolitan and even had its own gaming room. Since the three of them had been gambling pretty heavily, it made sense to stay in an establishment which catered for their needs in this respect. As Ryan said, they would be able to eat, drink and gamble the time away without having to set foot out of their hotel.

From time to time, Ryan went off just in the company of Lopez. It seemed to Tucker that the two other men thought that they were smarter than him and talked about their plans together, without him, because they thought him too slow to join in some of their conversations. He was quite right about this. Ryan got a little tired of having to explain even the simplest of details to the other members of their band and liked to plot things out alone or with Lopez from time to time. Today, they had gone off and told Tucker that he'd best fetch his things from the hotel that they were staying at and book into The Supreme, which was across town. They would pick up their own gear and join him there later.

Tucker didn't like dealing with the staff at hotels. He always had the impression that they were laughing up their sleeves at him, because he was often badly dressed and a little slow-spoken. So he'd delayed taking his things from the hotel they were at and transferring them to The Supreme. Instead, he'd wandered around town, visiting shops and having a few drinks here and there.

Now, Jack Tucker might be a little slower than the average man, but he had a marvellously tuned sense of danger. He did not have the vocabulary to put it into words, but he felt a little spooked today and was possessed of the notion that somebody was following him. Whether it was a guilty conscience or something else, Tucker had the idea that people were on his trail. This made it mighty tricky for Quincy to keep on the other man's tail, but he managed it, following Tucker all the way to the hotel where he and the others had been staying since they hit town.

When Tucker vanished into the hotel lobby, Quincy had to take a gamble on either waiting out there in the street or following the man inside. The fellow seemed jittery as anything already so Quincy decided to stand across the street for a spell, watching the front door of the hotel. Just as he was about to go in and start asking questions, Tucker emerged. He was still looking nervous and ill at ease. Although he had entered the hotel empty-handed, he was now carrying a carpet bag. Quincy's eyes narrowed. He'd bet $100 that Tucker had his share of the money in that bag.

Still maintaining a discreet distance, Quincy kept right after the man with the carpet bag. If he could only catch him alone in some less populous part of town, then he might be able to settle this business once and for all, by taking the money that he was sure Tucker was toting in that bag. The streets were packed, though, and Quincy didn't much take to the idea of being made the subject of a hue and cry. The matter was taken out of his hands.

Tucker had everything crammed into that old carpet bag; his spare shirt, shaving gear, spurs, box of ammunition, bottle of rye and of course twelve pounds' weight of gold coins. The fabric was frayed and weak and just as Tucker was crossing the road and about to enter the swanky new hotel where he was to book a room, disaster struck. There was a sudden ripping noise and the material of the carpet bag gave way; all Tucker's belongings fell out the bottom into the roadway, including hundreds of gold ten dollar pieces.

Even now, a man with a level head might have been able to retrieve the situation. Tucker wasn't up to it though. When the shining yellow coins cascaded into the road, Quincy caught his breath. His first impulse was to run forward and scoop up the money. Others had seen it though and there were shouts of amazement. At this juncture, Tucker did the worst thing imaginable. He pulled his gun and shouted to those staring at the gold, 'You all keep away now! This here's my money.'

It was such a peculiar and unexpected response to what was little more than a minor accident, that people began to look harder at Tucker, which in turn had the effect of making him still more flustered and anxious. One of the ten dollar pieces had rolled about fifteen feet away, behind Tucker. A passerby had bent down to pick it up; intending to take it over and return it to the unfortunate fellow

57

whose bag had ripped open. Out of the corner of his eye, Jack Tucker caught sight of the movement. Whirling round, he saw at once that the man had one of his gold pieces in his hand. Whether he was so keyed up that he simply twitched and pulled the trigger more or less accidentally, or if he had thought he was being robbed and acted to deter anybody else from grabbing at his wealth, nobody would ever discover. What happened was that there was a shot and the man who had picked up the ten dollar piece from the road, dropped dead with a bullet straight through his head.

There were cries of horror and the crowds swiftly moved back; some people throwing themselves to the ground. Tucker was trying to gather up the coins, but of course he was in such a panicked state, that as fast as he was picking up the money and shoving it in his bag, it all fell out again. Somebody shouted to fetch the sheriff and on hearing that word, Tucker looked up fearfully.

Augustus Birrell and Pete Owen were in a nearby street when they heard the gunshot. Birrell always investigated the sound of shooting. He couldn't help himself; it had become second nature during those decades when he had been a proper police detective. As the two of them reached the vicinity of The Supreme hotel, Birrel saw a crowd gathered at a wary distance around a man with a pistol in his hand. This person appeared to be fooling around with some bag, it was impossible at that distance to see what he was up to. As he led Owen nearer, the man said, 'I reckon that's one of 'em. One of the two who waited outside while I did that business with the gold coins.'

'You sure?' asked Birrell sharply.

'Yeah, I reckon.'

'Wait here for me, Owen. Don't bolt or you'll annoy me. I'm going to see what's what.'

The detective drew his revolver and moved cautiously forward. In the meantime, Tucker was still fumbling around, trying to fill up his bag again with the things which he had dropped.

It appeared to Quincy that there was very little that he could do except watch. If he went close to Tucker, he would certainly end up getting shot for his pains. The state of the man, he would like as not open fire on anybody who approached him. It was infuriating, because it was just as Quincy had suspected; Tucker had been carrying his share of the money in that old carpet bag. He was on the verge of ignoring all prudent considerations and moving in on the man anyway, when Quincy saw that somebody else was taking a hand in the drama. A smartly-dressed and respectable-looking man stepped out from the ring of spectators. He had in his hand a stubby little pistol.

'You best drop that gun,' said Birrell in a level, even voice, 'Otherwise, you're going to make things a whole lot worse for yourself.'

Jack Tucker paused from frantically attempting to pick up his gold and looked up at the man who had spoken. Tucker was holding both the carpet bag and his gun both in his right hand. He let fall the carpet bag and stood up slowly.

'Don't be a fool,' said Birrell, 'You can stop this now.' Even as he spoke, Birrell knew that it wasn't going to do any good and that this idiot was going to try and shoot his way out of trouble. The two of them were only about thirty feet apart and although Birrell's sawn-off pistol wasn't too accurate for long range, he reckoned that he should be able to take the fellow from here.

Jack Tucker made one final and very poor decision and then began raising his arm, with the clear intent of shooting the man who had challenged him. Birrell did not hesitate. He fired twice and Tucker crumpled to the ground. In a few paces, the detective was next to him and had snatched the revolver from unresisting fingers. Birrell stooped down to check on the man he had shot. He could see at once that it was all up with the fellow. He said, 'There's no time to fetch a priest or anything of that sort. You want to get straight with your God, then you best hurry, fella. You're like to be meeting him directly.'

A ring of bystanders and loafers had drawn round the two of them. Birrell said loudly and without turning round, 'I'm authorized to take charge of all that gold. Let me catch anybody taking one single coin and I'll have that man indicted for larceny.' He spoke with such assurance that nobody felt inclined to put the matter to the test. Quincy joined the sightseers and heard what the detective said. He examined the man curiously. It was the first time that it had crossed his mind that he himself might be in danger of having his neck stretched for his role in the robbery of the railroad train. He knew that he'd been part of their venture and wondered now if that made him jointly liable for the murder of Esther Hanigan. It would be ironic if he were to be arrested for the crime, now that he was doing everything in his power to make restitution to the dead woman's son.

Jack Tucker lay on the ground, his face clouded and bewildered. It was an expression often seen on his face during life, the world being a very confusing and puzzling sort of place to a man of such meagre intellect.

Birrell turned his eyes round the watching crowd and saw Quincy. For a moment, Quincy had the idea that the dying man was trying to frame some last words, but then his jaw went slack and his body stiffened for a moment and then relaxed utterly. The look on the dead man's face didn't change though, and Tucker was destined in death to wear that same slow-witted and uncomprehending expression that had been so characteristic of the man in life.

CHAPTER 5

The head of security for the Southern Pacific Railroad Company was feeling pretty braced with himself. His instincts had, as usual, proved sound and he had been quite right in supposing that the men who robbed the *Tucson Flyer* had chosen to come here to Yuma. He had accounted for one of the four and recovered almost a third of the gold which they had stolen. After tidying things up a little, Birrell had lodged the gold in a bank and then wired Tucson with the glad tidings. He had, almost by return, received fulsome congratulations from the directors of the railroad. This was a rare occurrence indeed, and indicated just how much store they must set by having this whole business cleared up.

Augustus Birrell lay on the bed in his hotel room, his hands clasped behind his head and a cheroot clenched in his teeth, fathoming matters out and putting together the pieces of the puzzle. When he first came to Yuma, he had been hunting for four men, but that had all changed now. In the first place, there was the indisputable fact that Pete Owen had only seen three men in total when he was changing that money for them. That didn't signify particularly, in itself; after all, the fourth man could have been making water round the back of the saloon for all he knew. More to the point though, the man he had killed had in his possession $3,468 in gold. This was a harder conundrum to solve, but Birrell thought he'd worked it out.

If those four robbers had divided up the money evenly, then each would have got around $3,000. A thousand dollars had been converted into paper money, leaving perhaps a little less than £2,700 for everybody. How come the dead man had some $700 more than that? The answer was easy. They hadn't shared the cash four ways, but three. That would tie in with Owen only seeing the three men. Somewhere down the line, those boys had dropped one of their number. It wasn't uncommon for thieves to fall out, of course. Birrell didn't care what had become of the other man; it just made his job a whole heap easier, he'd be going up against two men, instead of three.

While Birrell was lying on his bed, reasoning the case out to himself, Martin Quincy was one step ahead in the game. He now knew where the remaining members of the band were to be found and he made for their hotel, with a view to snatching back the money he was owed.

As soon as Tucker had breathed his last, the man who had shot him turned to the bystanders and demanded, 'Anybody know this man? Any of you can tell me where he's been staying?'

At once, Quincy could see that this was key to the whole thing. Wherever Tucker had been staying, that's where he'd be likely to find that other pair of skunks. Then a thought struck him. Looking at the contents of Tucker's bag, scattered there in the roadway, it looked like he'd been carrying everything with him. Was he leaving town? Moving to another hotel or what? Whatever it was, Quincy knew that he had an edge on this fellow who looked to be an official investigator. Because he alone knew which hotel Tucker had been removing his gear from, which was presumably the place where he had been staying with Ryan and Lopez. Without showing any particular haste, he turned away from the little tableau in the middle of the street and casually wandered back in the direction of the hotel which he had seen Tucker coming out of, not so very long before.

There was little time to lose; for all that Quincy knew to the contrary, the three men had been fixing on catching the next train west. That being so, he decided to adopt a direct method of approach and marched straight into the little hotel and went up to the clerk sitting behind the counter in the lobby. 'Say,' said Quincy, in a friendly tone of voice, 'I'm looking for a friend of mine. Rough looking party, wearing an old plaid shirt. Hear he's staying here.'

'That don't bring anybody to mind. We got more than one rough-looking type in a plaid shirt stopping here. Anything to mark him out?'

'Yes, I mind that he kept all his stuff in a carpet bag.'

'Oh, him!' said the clerk contemptuously. Then, recollecting that he might perhaps be talking to some relative or friend of the man in question, he moderated his tone somewhat and said, 'I know who you mean. He checked out just a short time back, I'm afraid.'

'Oh that's a real shame,' said Quincy, like Tucker had been his favourite brother or something of the sort, 'I so wanted to see him before he left town. You don't know, I suppose, where he was heading?'

'No, I don't. But hey, I tell you what. His two friends that he came here with are also leaving today. They might be able to help you.'

'Oh really? Do you happen to know where they might be found?'

'Yeah, you just missed them coming in. They passed by about thirty seconds before you did. They've gone up to their rooms to fetch their things. They're both booking out today as well. Just wait here and they'll be down directly.'

Of course, bumping into Ryan and Lopez like this, without any prior preparation, was the very last thing that Quincy wanted at that moment. At best, it would have set them on their guard; at worst, it could have precipitated a gunfight right here in the hotel. He said, 'Say, I just recalled some urgent business. I'll be right back.' With that, Quincy turned on his heel and fairly ran from the lobby, charging out into the street and being quickly lost to view among the crowds on the sidewalk.

The hotel clerk shook his head in amazement. 'Some folks!' he muttered to himself. One minute the fellow had been mad keen to find this friend of his, and then when he was told that those who most likely knew where he was were right there in the building, he bolted out into the street.

A few seconds later, Ryan and Lopez came down the stairs, carrying their leather bags. Ryan nodded at the clerk and said, 'We're all square, yeah?'

'Yes, sir, Mr Brown. You don't owe us a cent.' As Ryan moved towards the door, the clerk called out, 'There was a party looking for your friend, just left half a minute since.'

Ryan whirled round and strode up to the counter. He fixed the little clerk with eyes like gimlets and said softly, 'What did he look like? You tell me every last detail and don't leave nothing at all out.'

After wiring his bosses in Tucson and taking time out on his cot to figure out his next move, Birrell came to the conclusion that this was one of those cases where he was called upon to wear out shoe leather, making his inquiries in person. Police work was often like that. It had been a stroke of luck hearing that shot and stumbling across one of the gang in that way; he couldn't sit back on his behind and hope for another such bolt of lightning to strike. No, he'd have to manufacture his own luck from here on in.

So it was that Augustus Birrell, head of security for

the entire South Pacific line, fell back into the habits of his early professional life and began making door-to-door inquiries throughout Yuma. He knew that at least three of the bandits had been in town for a few days. They must have been staying somewhere; it was just a matter of finding out where. There was no directory for Yuma, the town was just too new for such a thing. Which meant that Birrell was forced to trudge up and down each and every street systematically looking for hotels and lodging houses.

Maybe a half hour after Ryan and Lopez left their hotel, and just when the clerk was breathing a little easier, following his fierce cross-examination by Ryan about the appearance of the fellow who had been asking after him, another man turned up, asking just exactly the same things.

At the first mention of a fellow wearing a plaid shirt and toting a carpet bag, the clerk said, 'He's gone and I don't rightly know where. Nor do I know where his friends have gone and I don't know aught about the other fellow asking a heap of questions neither. There, does that satisfy you?'

'Not hardly,' said Augustus Birrell and proceeded to question the clerk closely, under threat of vague and ill-defined legal penalties should that individual fail fully to co-operate. At the end of the quizzing though, Birrell was not a whit further advanced with his enquiries than he had been at the start. All he had managed to establish was that two friends of the man he had shot dead had been staying here in the company of the dead man, but had now left and nobody knew where they had gone. The hotel register was no help, it merely informed the detective that John Brown and Benito Juarez had been staying there from such and such a date until this very day.

'You didn't think it funny that a man calling himself by the same name as the president of Mexico should land up in your hotel?' asked Birrell.

'Not really,' said the clerk. In a sudden burst of frankness, he admitted, 'Folk staying here often use names that might not be strictly their own. What should I do about it, ask for proof of their identity?'

Augustus Birrell stared coldly at the man on the other side of the counter. 'Do not try to be funny with me,' he advised, 'It won't answer and will most likely end up with you getting into hot water. Drop it now.'

Patrick McFadden was pretty pleased with himself. Like Birrell, he was a salaried employee of the Southern Pacific Railroad Company but there the resemblance began and ended. Birrell, for all his rough ways and ruthless methods, was utterly straight and dedicated to his job. Patrick McFadden, on the other hand, had an eye only to the main chance. He would do anything at all which would turn him an extra buck.

McFadden's job was troubleshooter for the railroad. He travelled up and down the length of the line; dealing with problems, tracking down and putting an end to swindles and scams, and reducing the loss of revenue to the Southern Pacific caused by dishonest ticket clerks and greedy staff working on board the trains. In common with many of the larger undertakings at that time, the big railroad companies generally accepted losses of up to ten per cent through pilfering and dishonesty. They wrote off this ten per cent as 'shrinkage'. When the figure rose above ten per cent, action was usually taken.

The ones who had queered the pitch for the rest of the petty crooks working on the railroads were the men working the goods trains. The pickings there were so rich that the temptation to take just a little more on each journey had been proving irresistible. In the end, this resulted in the killing of the golden goose, when the head office in Tucson dispatched undercover investigators to see what could be done to reduce the losses.

McFadden was unknown to anybody else working for the Southern Pacific, other than one or two people at head office. Even Augustus Birrell would not have recognized him. This was essential, for one of McFadden's roles was to try and lure staff into committing acts of petty criminality. He would try and negotiate a long distance journey and see if the clerk would give him the ticket at a greatly reduced price. Such a transaction worked to the advantage of both parties. The man buying the ticket travelled cheap and sometimes the clerk pocketed the whole of this amount. The issuing of such irregular tickets really needed the co-operation of a conductor on the train, who would also expect a cut of the money thus generated.

It was Patrick McFadden who had passed on the tip to Ryan about the gold being carried from Tucson to Yuma, and he had profited from the provision of this information to the tune of $600. Since then, he had managed to cut himself in on some of the little rackets being operated by the railroad's staff here in Yuma. He had also picked up a juicy tidbit of information from official channels about a consignment of cash being brought down by road from Phoenix. It was this which had caused McFadden to attempt his most daring and audacious coup yet.

'What d'you make of it?' asked Ryan of Lopez, as they left the hotel at which they had been staying.

'Not the law, I think,' said the Mexican carefully, 'Else why would he run away when he hear that we're coming down?'

'No, I didn't think about the law. I suppose it could be him as I've been getting little bits of information from. Doesn't sound like him, though. We'd best keep our eyes peeled.'

The two men carried out this conversation in low voices as they made their way across the street, heading towards The Supreme Hotel. Quincy kept a good long distance between himself and the men he was following. He was most anxious not to be seen. If Ryan and Lopez knew that he was in Yuma, there was no telling how they would react. But one thing Quincy did know for sure was that those boys weren't carting all that gold about with them to every place that they went. Who in the hell would be wishing to carry ten or twelve pounds weight of heavy metal around wherever they went? It didn't make sense. Unless the two men were heading now to the depot, then they would without the shadow of a doubt be going somewhere that they could set down those bags. They wouldn't be sitting and watching them for twenty-four hours in the day, either. At some point, they would go off and leave their bags unattended and then would come his opportunity.

Seeing Tucker die and becoming aware that there was some kind of detective right here in Yuma who was evidently working to track down him and the others had come as somewhat of a shock to Quincy. Thinking it over, though, as he tailed Ryan and Lopez through the streets, he shouldn't really have been surprised. Twelve thousand dollars was a hell of a lot of money, and it stood to reason that the railroad company would want to recover it. This was the last thing that Quincy wanted to happen. If the rest of the money was to be taken back into the hands of the Southern Pacific, then the odds of a cent being used for the benefit of Esther Hanigan's orphaned son were vanishingly slender. By the most grotesque irony imaginable, he was the only person in the whole, entire world now who could do anything to help that child.

Ryan and Lopez seemed to know where they were going and once they had crossed the street, they walked straight through the doors of a very smart looking hotel, with a garish new sign at the front, just under the eaves, which announced that this was The Supreme Hotel. So that's all that it was, thought Quincy, they're just moving to a better class of establishment. Then a thought struck him. I wonder if they even know about Tucker being killed yet?

Neither of them were in the habit of booking hotel reservations ahead of time, both Ryan and the Mexican figuring that if they had the money, then it was up to the hotel to furnish them with the accommodation they required. They were in luck; The Supreme had a few single rooms free. Ryan said to the clerk, 'Friend of ours was due to book in here today. Man aged about thirty. Can you tell us what room he's in?'

'Nobody other than you gentlemen have booked in here this day,' said the fellow behind the counter, 'Maybe he's been delayed?'

'It could be so,' said Ryan, but when he and Lopez were heading up the stairs, he said, 'Where d'you suppose that lunkhead's got to now? Maybe we shouldn't let him wander round by himself like that.'

Now that he knew where Ryan was staying, all that remained was the small matter of separating him from that leather saddle-bag full of money that he had taken into the hotel. Quincy wasn't altogether sure right now how he was going to go about doing that. I guess, he thought, I'd best hang round here for a spell and see if either of those two scallywags comes out.

There was little enough chance though, of either Ryan or Lopez leaving the hotel for some good, long while; although Quincy couldn't have known this. As Ryan had remarked to the other two, The Supreme had everything that they could want, right there under its roof. What point would there be in traipsing through the streets, looking for card games and drinking dens, when the best in town were to be found only a few paces from their bedrooms? It was when they entered the bar-room, which doubled as a restaurant, that Ryan and Lopez found out about Tucker. It was the talk of practically every bar in Yuma that day, including that one.

Even before they got served, stray snatches of conversation could be heard.

'Right there in the middle of the street. . . .'

'Over $3,000 in gold. . . .'

'Say it's to do with that robbery, a while back. . . .'

'Shot a fellow as just picked up one o' them coins. . . .'

Although he could pretty well work out for himself what might have chanced, Ryan asked the barkeep outright, as he was pouring them a beer, 'What's this everybody seems to be talkin' of? There been some shooting?'

'Yes, sir, you might say so. Two men killed stone dead. Only a block away from here.'

'Anybody know what it was all about?'

The man shrugged as he took Ryan's money. 'Couldn't rightly say, 'cept that there was a heap o' gold picked up afterwards. Folk are saying as it was something to do with that hold-up, up towards Tucson. Train got robbed.'

'Oh yeah,' said Ryan, 'I seem to recollect reading something of the sort.'

When they were seated at a table, out of earshot of the other customers, Lopez said quietly, 'That mean we got to take this stage by ourselves, huh?'

'Not so loud, you damned fool,' said Ryan sharply, 'Just keep your voice down. What's the matter, you afeared to knock over a stage, just you and me?'

The Mexican flashed his teeth in genuine amusement. 'I, afraid? I don't think so. But will need thought, no?'

'That it will. It's a damned nuisance. Lord knows what Tucker was thinking of to get his self shot like that.'

McFadden was due to meet up with Ryan in two hours. He had a number of things to do before then. When he had passed on the information about the shipment of gold being carried on the *Tucson Flyer*, McFadden had been content to wait until after the robbery had been committed, before taking his five per cent. This time, he was playing things a little differently. He was reasonably confident that nobody else in this part of the territory knew the exact time that the stage would be coming south from Phoenix with the money for the banks here in Yuma. That meant that the information he was selling was at a premium.

If he had been asked, Patrick McFadden would have said, and what's more, genuinely believed, that he was not a greedy man. All he wanted was a few hundred dollars over and above his salary. He could live comfortably enough on the money that the Southern Pacific paid him, but if he wanted anything more than just making do comfortably; then he had to provide the wherewithal himself. He had made $600 from the information about the gold coming to Yuma and now he aimed to make another four hundred from selling the details of the cash being transferred to the banks here. That would mean that he had made $1,000 in just two weeks. That would be enough to content him for a while yet. Why, he thought to himself, a greedy man would have tried for twice that! When carrying out these calculations, McFadden generally found it easier on his conscience not to include the backhanders and pay-offs that he took from the crooked staff on the railroad. He regarded that as pin money; hardly worth factoring in when he was totalling up his financial affairs.

The next day, McFadden was travelling back to Tucson, and since neither Ryan nor the other group of men he was dealing with knew his real name or what position he held, he didn't think that he need fear any repercussions from what he did here, coming after him in the future and biting his behind. Even so, Ryan and Lopez were still loose ends and although the odds were a million to one against it, there was still the faint nagging worry at the back of McFadden's mind that they would come across him again in the future, and that his role in the robbery of the train might come back to haunt him. Maybe they would try and put the bite on him and blackmail him or some such. It was this fear which had prompted his latest money-making scheme.

Truth to tell, Patrick McFadden was pleased as punch with himself about the latest scheme of his devising. In less than an hour, he was meeting a man who had been put in touch with him by somebody working on the railroad. This fellow was, although this had not been explicitly stated, a road agent; a man who would hold up stages or even individual travellers, if they looked as though they were worth enough. He and a couple of friends operated just exactly like the old-time highwaymen in England, a hundred years ago. McFadden was going to sell to this man, for $200, the time and route of the stage-coach bringing the cash to Yuma the next day.

Apart from doubling the money he received for this information, it was clear that the scene would be set for a three way fight between the armed guards on the stage and two parties of bandits. With a little good fortune, Ryan and his men would be killed in the ensuing gun battle and that would be a weight indeed off McFadden's mind. After all, it was exceedingly unlikely that any of the participants in the fighting would be sitting around afterwards and exchanging notes about where their information had come from.

There was one last point which McFadden hadn't mentioned to either of the men from whom he was receiving $200 and that was this. In addition to a couple of men riding shotgun on top of the stage, there was going to be a half dozen others riding inside; all of them armed to the teeth with the latest repeating rifles. The chances of any of those bandits escaping with their lives was as slim as you could hope for.

CHAPTER 6

The head of security for the Southern Pacific Railroad Company was still trudging round the streets of Yuma in his patient and methodical way, trying to find where the remnants of the gang which he was after might be hiding themselves. It might be thought that a man of such present eminence as Augustus Birrell would feel humiliated and demeaned by making door-to-door inquiries in this way, like some rookie on the beat in a big city. Fact was, he found it relaxing and not in the least disagreeable. It was just like the old days and made him feel like a young man.

Having exhausted all the cheaper flophouses and dives, Birrell was working his way through the classier joints. He didn't see it likely that the men he sought would be holed up in The Supreme, but he knew that he had to cover every possibility. That was what police work was all about. So it was that about eight that evening, having checked nigh on all the other places in town, he made for The Supreme

Hotel, where Ryan and Lopez were drinking in the bar.

Now, if Birrell had moved just a little more quickly and been a tad less thorough in the questions he had been asking in all those other lodging houses, then a great deal of bloodshed might have been prevented and several lives saved. He wasn't, of course, to know that this was one of those cases where a few minutes either way could make all the difference in the world. As it was, he got to The Supreme at just the wrong moment.

Ryan and Lopez had sat in the bar of The Supreme, getting pretty well liquored up for the better part of two hours. Lopez became garrulous and expansive when in his cups, but Ryan simply grew meaner and meaner. However drunk he might be, he was still able to function well enough, to the extent of throwing an accurate punch and shooting straight. And even worse was the indisputable fact that while some men become friendly and good-natured when drunk, others grow dangerously aggressive. That was how the drink took Ryan.

'I hate this kind of joint!' said Ryan. 'Folk all dressed so smart and looking down their noses at men like us.'

Lopez looked around the room in surprise. 'There ain't nobody looking bad at you. Is the drink speaking. You are mistook.'

The Mexican's grasp of idiomatic English might not have been wonderful, but he had surely summed up the case neatly. Nobody had even noticed the two

79

scruffy men sitting at the table, a little apart from everybody else.

'You say what?' asked Ryan, truculently. 'You sayin' I'm wrong? Or maybe you think I'm a liar?'

Lopez was used to the sudden and unexpected changes of mood to which his companion was prone and knew that unless the aggression could be deflected on to a third party, Ryan was perfectly capable of erupting in violence which would be directed against his partner. Far better, thought Lopez, to direct this smouldering anger elsewhere.

'No, no, my friend, I don't say you are wrong. You know these sorts of men better than I. What do I know about it? You think they laugh at us behind our back, is that it?'

Mollified a little, Ryan said, 'Yeah, look at that bastard there, the one with the sideburns. See how he looks at us out the corner of his eye, like we got no business here.'

'You speak truly,' said Lopez, vastly relieved to see the focus of Ryan's anger changing, 'I thought the same thing my own self.'

The man in question, a hulking great fellow who worked as a haulier, became aware that the two men on another table were staring at him and discussing his appearance. He turned around and stared right back at them. Neither the white man nor the Mexican averted their gaze and after a few seconds, he said in a loud enough voice to carry across the bar, 'You boys have something to say, you best come right out with it. 'Less you're too yellow to speak plain to a fellow's face, that is.'

Although The Supreme was angling to become a swanky sort of place where wealthy Easterners would stay when they were travelling to California and so on, for now they had the same, often rough, type of clientele as the other, cheaper hotels in Yuma. Many of these men were not at all disinclined to brawl after having imbibed a certain amount of intoxicating liquor, and although The Supreme had only opened less than six months previously, they had already experienced a number of ferocious roughhouses in their bar-room.

Neither Ryan nor Lopez said anything in response to the man with the sideburns' words, but just continued to sit there, staring insolently at him. This was quite enough and the man got to his feet and said, 'You boys really beginning to tick me off. You want to step outside, or settle it right here and now?' As he stood up, the two men drinking with him, who had only made his acquaintance that very evening in the bar, felt honour-bound to get up and stand by his side.

It was Ryan who set the match to the powder train, by lurching to his feet and picking up the unoccupied chair next to his own. This he shied at the man with the sideburns, who managed to fend it away; where it landed on a table covered with drinks. This caused the men around that table to join the fray and in next to no time at all, the whole bar was a seething mass of furious, drunk men throwing punches and pieces of furniture at each other. The clerk came in to see what the deuce was going on, and was unfortunate enough to be hit by a chair which had just been thrown. He keeled over, knocked unconscious by the impact.

It was at this very moment that Augustus Birrell walked through the doors of The Supreme, seeking information about any recent guests who might match the description of two men for whom he was hunting. He could see at once that there was some species of disturbance. Staff from the hotel were running into the bar and one man was carried out, unconscious and his face covered in blood.

'I'm sorry to trouble you folk at such a time,' said Birrell, catching the arm of one of those who was carrying the limp body, 'But I've a few questions about two men who might have booked into your hotel today.'

'Fella, you'll have to come back another time,' said the harassed individual whose sleeve he had hold of. 'As you can see, we're mighty busy right now.'

'If I could just speak to the clerk who books folk in?' said Birrell.

'This here's the man you want, but as you can see, he ain't a-goin' to be answering no questions for a spell yet. He's been knocked out. Now if you'll excuse me. . . .'

Birrell knew when an enterprise was hopeless and this present case fitted the bill to a T. He doubted if the man being carried out of the bar would be in fit state to answer his questions until the next morning at the very earliest. He reluctantly let go of the man's arm and turned on his heel. He would just have to wait 'til tomorrow before asking any more questions at this hotel.

McFadden was pleased with himself. He only wished that there was somebody that he could share his satisfaction with. The man he'd met an hour ago had cheerfully handed over $200 for the details about the stage heading to Yuma from Phoenix. All that remained now was to meet Ryan and sell him the self-same bit of information for a similar sum and then he, Patrick McFadden, would be home and dry. Knowing that you were cheating one person was a mighty good feeling inside, but the knowledge that you were cheating two or three people at the same time was something else again. It surely was a pity that he would never be able to laugh about this with anybody.

When Ryan showed up in the alleyway near the livery stable, McFadden was shocked at the sight of him. The man's hair was tangled and matted with some dark liquid and his face had several grazes down one side. It was hard to tell in the light of the moon, but McFadden had the impression that there was also the beginnings of a black eye.

'Lord, what happened to you, man? You look terrible!'

'Don't you worry none 'bout me,' growled Ryan, 'I'll do well enough. What about you? You got what I want?'

'Yeah, for sure. Where's the money? You know what we agreed this time.'

'You'll take it in gold pieces?'

'Are you crazy?' exclaimed McFadden in horror. 'I don't want to so much as touch one o' them coins. No, you pay me in paper bills and that'll be fine.'

'It don't much signify anyway,' grunted Ryan and if Patrick McFadden had been just a little less cock-sure of himself, he might have wondered at this statement. He was so confident of his ability to take care of his own affairs though, that the nuance escaped him. Ryan laughed and handed over some folded bank notes, saying, 'You best count them. Don't want you to say I cheated you.'

'That's all right. Now listen and I'll tell you about the plans for tomorrow.'

It took only three or four minutes for McFadden to fill in the other man on what he needed to know. Ryan nodded appreciatively. 'That's all that me and my partner need to know. I am right obliged to you.'

Now the problem with trying to pull a fast one on somebody in a business deal is that you never quite know when the other fellow might have just the same intention towards you. For McFadden, Ryan was a loose end that needed to be tidied away. The neatest way of achieving that end was to see the man killed, which was what he hoped the end result of the next day's adventures would be for Ryan and his companion in crime. It did not cross McFadden's mind for a fraction of a second that Ryan himself might have seen him in just that same light; as a potential, future hazard to be disposed of now, in order to avoid an embarrassment at a later date. McFadden could positively identify Ryan, and was the sort of craven dog as might turn state's evidence if the going got tough, just to save his own skin. Better by far to do away with that risk in the future, be it ever so slender.

Reaching out his hand to shake on the deal, believing that the man whose hand he was about to take would be dead within twenty-four hours, Patrick McFadden was hugely surprised when instead of putting his own right hand out, Ryan grabbed McFadden's wrist with his left hand and reached into his jacket. The realization of his danger dawned at the very same moment that the man in front of him plunged a narrow bladed dagger into the railroad employee's chest. Then Ryan withdrew the blade and slashed McFadden's throat; moving back almost immediately, to avoid being fouled by the sudden gush of blood. He let McFadden fall lifeless into the dirt and then reached down and wiped the knife clean on the dead man's pants. Then he sheathed his blade and walked briskly back to the hotel.

Pete Owen had quickly vanished in the aftermath of Jack Tucker's death. Birrell had been a little pre-occupied of late, what with trying not to get killed and so on. By the time he'd got matters in hand, Owen had skipped off, the Lord knew where. This was annoying, because he was the only person in the whole of Yuma, as far as Birrell was aware, who could provide a positive identification of the men who'd ambushed the *Tucson Flyer*. Augustus Birrell was no slouch when it came to winkling out men who, whether from natural shyness or for some other reason, are reluctant to be found. He had tracked down Owen's home, checked his bar a dozen times; all without any luck. After being thwarted in his desire to interview the clerk at The Supreme, Birrell decided that he would find Owen for sure this night.

The housekeeper at Owen's clapboard house on the edge of town was a slatternly mulatto, who was at first hesitant about allowing her master's home to be searched. She relented when Birrell produced a couple of five dollar bills. 'I don't know nothin' 'bout it, I'm sure,' said the woman, 'Master ain't been here since yesterday morn. I can't say where he's gone. Odd times, he vanish for a week, a month. He don't tell me nothin'.'

It didn't take Birrell long to see that the woman was telling the truth. There was no sign of Owen. I'll cut his balls off and wear 'em on my watch-chain, thought Birrell, I knew that son of a bitch would disappear at the first opportunity. Shoulda handcuffed him to a hitching post when I took on that fella in the highway.

'Tell your master that Mr Birrell was searching for him. Think you can do that?'

'Yessir, I reckon as I can do that. Shall I tell him what you was askin' after him for?'

'He'll know,' said Birrell shortly.

After leaving Owen's home, the detective headed across to the missing man's bar for a final time.

There were no lights on and the place didn't look to Birrell's practiced eye as though anybody had been there since last he had peered through the window, at about midday. He tried the door, which was bolted from within. He looked up and down the street, which looked to be quiet and more or less deserted. Without making too much of it, Birrell turned round to survey the street, pulling out his gold half-hunter and checking the time, as though he was expecting somebody. Then he jabbed his elbow sharply backwards; dislodging a pane of glass from the door to the bar.

Once he was sure that nobody was watching, Birrell reached through the space where the glass had been and unbolted the door. Then he slipped inside the little saloon and bolted the door behind him. He didn't want to advertise his presence by lighting a match so he shuffled across the room in the dark. Birrell could just about make out the outlines of the tables well enough to steer his course around them. He worked on the assumption that the floor itself should be clear of obstacles and it was this which caused him to come crashing to the floor. What it was he had tripped over, Birrell had no idea at all. It felt soft and yielding, but at the same time heavy. His best guess was a rolled up carpet. 'The hell with it,' Birrell muttered to himself, 'Worth risking a light, I reckon. Otherwise, I'm apt to break my neck, blundering round in the dark like this.'

As soon as the sulphurous light of the Lucifer flared up and illuminated the room, Birrell could see at once just what it was he had stumbled over. It was Pete Owen's corpse, lying on its back, with the eyes open, staring lifelessly at the smoke-begrimed ceiling of his tavern. It wasn't the first time that Augustus Birrell had found himself alone in a darkened room with a dead body, so he didn't waste any time crossing himself, praying for the dead man's repose or any such foolishness. Instead, he reached over and flipped open Owen's jacket, looking for a bullet or knife wound.

Pete Owen had been killed with a single stab-wound to his heart. It was one of the neatest and most economical murders that Birrell had ever seen. The killer had stabbed the man once, withdrawn his blade and then waited until he dropped to the floor, before bending down and wiping the blade clean on his victim's trousers. Leastways, this was what it looked like to the detective as he ran his eyes over the corpse. How come the door was bolted on the inside was the next question which struck Birrell, and a quick look into the pantry at back of the counter soon solved that little mystery. The window there was closed, but the catch not fastened on the inside. He supposed that after murdering the owner of the saloon, the killer had climbed out of that rear window and then just pushed it behind him.

The only problem now was to figure out whether or not this death was a consequence of Owen's helping him, or if it was purely a coincidence. A man like Pete Owen had his fingers in many crooked pies; it wouldn't be hugely surprising if a number of people wanted him dead. Birrell concluded that there was no way that he would ever be able to decide the question definitely, one way or the other. He accordingly dismissed it from his mind. It really was a damned nuisance though. His only witness gone.

Although Birrell never found this out, Pete Owen was just one more loose end that Ryan thought was better tucked out of the way. He had killed Owen earlier that evening, before the fight in The Supreme. There was now only one man in Yuma who knew Ryan's face and that was Quincy.

For the last fifteen years, Martin Quincy's conscience had been more or less inactive. He had got up to so many dubious and downright crooked things since the end of the war, that most observers would not have bet a dime on Quincy still retaining even the least vestige of the conscience with which he had been born. Perhaps it was determined to make up for lost time, because Quincy's conscience was surely giving him hell now. Whatever the explanation and despite remaining idle for so many years, that conscience of his was currently pounding away like a beam engine working at full capacity.

It was now almost eleven and there was nothing more that he could do to advance his object today. A while ago, Quincy had walked past The Supreme, scouting it out to see if he might have a chance to slip up into Ryan or Lopez's room to take the gold that he knew was there. There had been an almighty ruckus going on there, though, and through the window, he could see Ryan in the thick of it. As Quincy weighed up the pros and cons of trying to find out what rooms the two men were in, a couple of deputies arrived, clearly with the intention of putting a stop to the fighting. There didn't seem to be anybody minding the counter either, so for both those reasons, he chose to give it a miss for that day.

The longer that he was compelled to delay, the more chance there was of that child being shipped off to the orphans' asylum; at least if what had been reported in that newspaper was correct. Quincy had an idea that handing over a large sum of money for the upkeep of the boy would prove a good deal easier if he was treating with the child's aunt, than if he had to explain himself to the superintendent of an orphanage. Tomorrow, he would face down Ryan and Lopez, come what may. If they wouldn't co-operate, well then Quincy would just shoot the pair of them. They were a worthless couple of scoundrels, when all was said and done and not likely to be any great loss to the world. Be that as it may, tomorrow was the day, or his name wasn't Martin Quincy.

CHAPTER 7

Ryan and Lopez had adjoining rooms in The Supreme. The management wasn't able to get to the bottom of the disturbance the previous night; otherwise the two of them might have been thrown out. As it was, the deputies restored order and a number of drinkers who were not resident in the hotel were pitched out into the street.

Lopez woke first and was delighted to see that it was a bright, sunny day. The Mexican was a simple and uncomplicated soul. Although he had a callous disregard for human life when the occasion demanded, as he had amply demonstrated during the raid on the railroad train, Lopez didn't enjoy killing and injuring people in the way that Ryan did. For Lopez, such activities were a necessary part of his work; for Ryan they were in the nature of a perk, something which gave an added fillip to a robbery. It was for this reason that Lopez was wondering if the time had not perhaps come when he should simply slip away and leave Ryan to find a new partner.

You would need to be blind not to notice how high the turnover was in Ryan's criminal associates. In the last few weeks, Lopez had seen both Tucker and Quincy fall by the wayside. He also suspected, but had no particular motive for looking any deeper into the matter, that Ryan had killed the fellow who had supplied him with his information. Fact was, the life expectancy of those working with Ryan was fairly low.

Well, there was the job today, which was already set up. He would ride with Ryan on this and then see how his thoughts were running at the end of the day. One thing was very certain in Lopez's mind. If he was going to leave Ryan, then he would do so without any warning. Quincy's fate was still fresh in his mind.

As he lay on his back musing in this way, the Mexican was suddenly aware that he was being watched. He turned his head to see that Ryan had already awoken and entered his room while Lopez was still sleeping. And what was more, he was staring at him balefully. Lopez chose to ignore this, smiling broadly and saying, 'Is a beautiful morning, no? You must have crept in here like a cat.'

Ryan scowled and said, 'What the hell do you care if it's a beautiful morning? What, you want to go an' paint the scene in water colours?'

It seemed safer to keep quiet and see what was said next. Ryan found the stub of a cigar which he had been smoking the previous night, lit it and smoked in silence for a space. At last he said, 'We'd best be moving soon. We got a fair ride this morning. I don't want that we should take that stage too close to town. I don't want any o' those deputies getting mixed up in the business.'

'Sure. Soon as you like.'

After another longish pause, Ryan said, 'I don't know 'bout you, Lopez, but I ain't fixin' to leave my money here in this room for any nosy cow's son to chance upon. I'm taking it with me.'

Lopez considered this statement. It sounded to him as though Ryan did not have it in mind to return to Yuma. If so, why didn't he just say so outright? Lopez had a very finely attuned sense of danger and he could feel the hairs prickling on the back of his neck now. It was like when lightning is about to strike. Was it in Ryan's mind to ride out with him this day and then shoot him in the back and take his money, the way that he had taken Quincy's share?

'For my part, I will leave my money here,' said Lopez. 'I am returning. I will tell the hotel to hold this room.'

Ryan and Lopez had a light breakfast; what The Supreme was pleased to call a French Breakfast.

'Stuck up bastards,' said Ryan irritably, 'Why can't they just call it a coffee and roll? What the hell's France got to do with the case?' He really was, thought Lopez to himself, in a vile mood this morning.

Elsewhere in Yuma, Augustus Birrell and Martin Quincy were also eating breakfast. Quincy was staying in a modest little boarding house in the older part of town. He was determined that he would get hold of what he thought of as 'his' share of the gold today and then light out at once for Maricopa Wells. He hoped that he could accomplish this without bloodshed, but he really was in a hurry now.

Birrell had now inquired of every hotel in Yuma bar one. That one was The Supreme and as he drank his coffee, he acknowledged to himself that the men he sought were almost certainly staying there. He blamed himself for starting at the cheaper places. He should have thought that men of that type, when they had a few dollars in their pockets, were always anxious to spend their money as soon as possible. Of course they would stay in the most expensive place in town.

Quincy and Birrell missed the men that, for very different reasons, they both wished to interview, by a matter of fifteen minutes or so. Quincy was actually standing behind Birrell in the hotel lobby while the detective asked the clerk about his guests.

'Two fellows of about thirty, thirty-five, you say?' said the young man behind the counter, 'Well, sir, our usual man isn't at work today. There was a regular shindy here last night. . . .'

'Yes, yes,' said Birrell hastily, 'I know all about that. Just tell me what you do know.'

'Well, sir, there were two fellows who might match your description. Foreign-looking gentleman and a white man. They had breakfast here this morning.'

'You're a wordy bastard,' said Birrell coarsely,

'Where are they now?'

'Left, sir,' said the fellow, not taking overmuch to being described in such terms. 'Booked out and headed the Lord knows where. Sorry I can't help you further.'

Birrell muttered an oath under his breath and left the hotel without saying another word.

'He's a right charmer!' remarked Quincy to the young man after Birrell had stormed off. The young-ster had reddened when the brusque man had called him a bastard and now felt that he could let his feelings show a little.

'Did you ever hear the like?' he said indignantly. 'I don't believe that anybody has ever talked to me so in my whole life. Good manners cost nothing.'

'What do you suppose he wanted with those men he was asking after?' said Quincy casually.

'I couldn't say. If he'd waited a little longer and been a mite more courteous, I could have told him that they're probably coming back this afternoon.'

'Is that a fact?'

'Yes, they said to hold their rooms. Left a deposit to secure them too. I'm jiggered if I'm going to go charging after that fellow to tell him, though not after the way I was spoke to. Anyways, how may I help you, sir?'

'I might want a room for tonight, but I just recalled that I have something urgent to attend to.' Upon saying which, Quincy too hurried out of The Supreme without bidding the other man farewell. The fellow behind the counter was beginning to think that it was going to be one of those days.

Ryan and Lopez rode along side by side in uneasy silence. Lopez was keeping a close eye on his partner and making damned sure that he did not get too far ahead of the other man. He knew that Ryan was not such a one as to exhibit any scruples about shooting a man in the back and he surely was not about to put the matter to the test. Every time that Ryan slowed down, so too did Lopez. Whether Ryan noticed this, it was impossible to say. After they had ridden in complete silence for maybe thirty minutes, Ryan said, 'I didn't know better, I'd say you was nervy.'

'Not to worry about my nerves. They are steady.'

'You still game for goin' after this stage?'

'That's why we come here, no?'

'You know, Lopez,' said Ryan, 'I hope you ain't vexed with me or nothin'. Job like this present one, we got to watch each other's backs.'

Upon hearing Ryan talk of watching his back, the Mexican shot his companion a sharp look, which Ryan met innocently. Lopez said, 'How far to where we are to attack this famous stagecoach?'

'Three miles, maybe. We need to talk tactics. Let's rein in for a spell.'

'What will you have?'

'There's only the two of us. I'm not minded to hold up this coach in the usual way.'

'I don't make you out,' said Lopez, 'What are you meaning?'

'It's easy enough. I don't mean to challenge the driver of the coach and ask him to stop. There's two men riding shotgun, one front and one back. Given the odds, they might want to make a fight of it. After all, we've only pistols and they goin' to have the best up-to-date rifles. No, it's too risky.'

'What then?'

'Why, we just ride up and greet them, give 'em the time of day and so on. Like we're just chance travellers on the road. Once we pass them, we wheel round and go after them shooting. We'll try and kill the driver and his guards before they know that anything's amiss.'

It sounded like cowardly and cold-blooded murder, but Lopez found this oddly reassuring. Ryan would hardly wish to increase the odds against him in such a venture by killing the only other man riding with him this day. That meant that at least until they had killed the men on the stage, there wasn't much chance of Ryan wishing to shoot him in the back. After the robbery had been accomplished; ah, then they would see. But for now. . . .

Lopez smiled gaily at his partner and said, 'We are friends, no? Friends should trust one another. Come!' And he rode off ahead of Ryan, no longer thinking that the other might put a bullet in his back.

Back in Yuma, Augustus Birrell and Martin Quincy were both engaged in rather different occupations. Quincy was simply watching the front entrance to The Supreme hotel. He couldn't of course just stand outside like a sentry; scanning the faces of those who went in and out of the place.

Instead, he was strolling up and down the street, first on one side and then on the other, but never once taking his eyes from the door to the hotel. He'd no idea at all if Ryan and his Mexican friend would even return there today, but it was the only chance he had of catching up with the two men and so he stuck at it manfully.

Over at the sheriff's office, the detective from the railroad company was having a somewhat trying interview with the local sheriff. As the counter clerk at The Supreme had noticed, Birrell never bothered with any of the usual conventions, either socially or professionally. When an investigator like him arrived in a town, it was considered courteous and proper for such a man to report at his earliest convenience to the local sheriff or police and just let them know that he was operating on their territory. Birrell hadn't bothered to abide by this convention and Charlie Nugent, the sheriff, was not a little displeased with him. Nugent's irritation was in no way assuaged, when almost the first thing that the head of security for the railroad company told him was that he had stumbled across a dead body the night before, and was only now reporting it to the duly appointed authorities.

'You and me sat here in this office just a short time back,' said Sheriff Nugent bluntly. 'You told me who you was, but didn't say anything about pursuing enquiries here. You shot that fellow and represented it to me as being more or less a chance occurrence, like you just tripped over him on the highway. You didn't say a damned word about coming here to my town to make your investigations. How's that?'

Birrell considered for a moment before replying. Then he said, 'I guess I like to play my cards close to my chest.'

This answer did not endear him to the sheriff, who said, 'If you get smart with me, Birrell, I'll lock you up right this moment as a material witness and possible suspect in the murder of Pete Owen. Is that plain enough for you?'

'That it is,' said Birrell.

'Sure?'

'Yeah. I'm sure.'

'Well then,' said Sheriff Nugent, 'Maybe now you'd like to explain to me just how you came to break into Pete Owen's tavern, and why, and list all your dealings with him. Then you can tell me if you think you caused his death in any way at all.' Nugent called out to one of his deputies, 'Hey, Rob! Set a pot of coffee goin'. This looks like being a long morning.'

The land hereabouts was gritty and didn't much favour vegetation of any kind, other than some scrubby patches of course grass and the occasional cactus. The road to Phoenix passed beneath a towering escarpment, which ran along to Ryan and Lopez's right-hand side as they rode north. There were not many other travellers on the road that morning. Once in a while, they passed some lone rider heading down to Yuma, but apart from that, nothing at all. Ahead of them, they could see three riders going in the same direction as themselves, whom they were gradually overtaking.

'How long, you think, 'til we meet this coach?' asked Lopez.

Ryan glanced up to the clear blue sky. 'I calculate, from what I been told, that our paths should cross at about midday.'

'It's not far off that now,' observed the Mexican, anxiously scanning the distant horizon.

'You're too impatient, Lopez. You always was. It'll be the death o' you one of these fine days.'

'You think so?'

'Hold fast,' said Ryan, 'Is that dust I can see over yonder?'

The two of them reined in their horses and stared into the distance. There was a tiny smudge of grey, just about as far ahead as they could see. It looked like the cloud of dust and grit which might be kicked up by a team of four horses pulling a heavy stage-coach. Without saying a word to each other, both Ryan and Lopez spurred on their mounts towards the oncoming stage. There was only one unexpected feature of the affair so far, and that was that it looked likely that they might reach their target at about the same time as the three riders ahead of them, who also looked to have increased their speed. But unless those others turned out to be lawmen, an exceed-ingly unlikely turn of events, they could be left out of the equation. Ordinary folk, even if they witness a robbery or murder, very seldom feel it worthwhile hazarding their own lives by interfering. The worst that would happen was that if the crime were to seen by those men ahead, then they would gallop off to Phoenix to raise the alarm. By the time any posse from Phoenix set out after them, Ryan and Lopez would be many miles away.

The morning wore on slowly and painfully for Birrell. Sheriff Nugent was being as painstaking and thorough as he had every right to be, and although it was a great personal inconvenience to him, the railroad detective bore the man no animosity. He would have acted just the same when he'd been a police officer in Chicago, if some unofficial person had been stirring up the mud in his district.

About noon, somebody came to the office to report the finding of another corpse, over near the livery stable. It was the body of a young man, which had escaped notice because it lay in a narrow and ill-frequented alleyway between two buildings. According to the fellow who reported it, there was so much blood, it looked like the boy had had his throat cut.

'Don't suppose you know anything about this, do you, Mr Birrell?' asked the sheriff politely. 'Only this is the third violent death in as many days.'

'What, you're minded to connect me with every unsolved crime in your town? I told you, why don't you wire the Southern Pacific, they'll vouch for me.'

'All in good time,' said Nugent. 'In the meanwhile, you just set here with Rob and carry on writing out your statement. Be sure to leave out nothing which might be, as the lawyers say, "germane to the issue at hand", neither.'

Quincy was getting mighty sick of patrolling this little stretch of the street, back and forth and then back again. He rather thought that some of those he had passed a few times as they moved from store to store, were giving him strange looks like they might have noticed that he wasn't really doing anything, other than walk backwards and forwards along that same short distance.

It was about midday and Quincy was wondering whether or not he could risk taking a break from his self-imposed tour of duty. He rather thought not. It would only take a matter of seconds for the men he was seeking to slip through the door of the hotel and be lost from sight. There was nothing for it, he would just have to stick at it. It was a good thing that he'd made sure to have a hearty breakfast.

The sheriff examined carefully the body lying in the mud of the alley. It was that of a young man, who could have been no more than twenty-five years of age. He'd bled like a stuck hog from having his throat slashed, so it was hard to tell if there were any other marks upon the body. The front of his clothes was saturated in blood. Nugent was looking for something though, and carefully flipped aside the jacket and peered closely at the shirt covering the corpse's chest. And there it was! A neat little slit in the material of the shirt-front which told him that this youngster had been stabbed in the front first, before having his throat cut. Knifings of this sort were not common in Yuma. Most of those who were killed by stabbing, tended to die as a result of bar-room brawls. It was strange to find two hole-and-corner murders by this method; both taking place within a few hours of each other.

Sheriff Nugent searched the body, taking care not to get any blood on his own clothes. His wife complained like mad when she had to deal with bloodstains. There was over $200 in the inside jacket pocket, which was quite a largish sum to be carrying around. There was also a bunch of keys and a folded sheet of expensive-looking writing paper. He extracted this from the pocket and then stood up to read it.

Well, thought Nugent to himself, after he had thoroughly absorbed the contents of the document – which he had taken from the dead man's pocket – this is a facer and no mistake! He thought wrathfully of that fellow Birrell, sitting back in his office, foxing with him for half the morning. If I don't have him arraigned on a conspiracy charge before the day's out, thought Nugent, Mr Augustus Birrell and me are going to have to have a straight conversation and lay our cards down on the table.

When he got back to his office, Sheriff Nugent didn't waste any time, but simply took out the sheet of paper and handed it to Birrell, saying, 'Would you care to explain this to me?' Birrell read the letter. It was written in flowing, copper-plate handwriting below the imposing heading of the Southern Pacific Railroad Company, and it confirmed that Patrick McFadden was a confidential agent of that company and requested that all law enforcement agencies in the territory of Arizona should be cognizant of this fact, and afford the bearer of the letter any assistance that he might require.

'Well,' said the sheriff, when Birrell had finished reading, 'What do you have to say about that?'

'Only that I never heard this fellow's name before this day. It's news to me that he's in town. Where is he? I might perhaps recognize him if I could meet him to speak to.'

'That'll hardly be possible, Mr Birrell. Condition that young man's in, I wouldn't have thought as he's going to be speaking to many people today.'

'Is he injured?'

'He's dead, Birrell. The man who was carrying that letter of introduction in his pocket is lying stone dead in an alley over by the livery stable. You best stop fooling with me now, for I'll not have it any more. If you don't tell me every last detail of who you are and what you're up to in my town, then before God, I'll clap you in a cell and you can sit there until you feel a little more talkative.'

It didn't appear to the railroad detective that he had another choice. He said, 'All right. Here's how things stand. . . .'

CHAPTER 8

By the time that they could make out the red paint-work of the stage heading towards them, it was clear to Ryan and Lopez that they would most likely reach their target at the same moment as the three riders ahead of them. Although they didn't say it out loud to each other, both Ryan and the Mexican were thinking the same thing; that it might prove necessary to kill those three men, as well as the crew of the stagecoach. As they drew nearer, though, this looked an unattractive prospect, because the closer they came to overtaking the men in front of them on the road, the more obvious it became that those men were heavily armed and might not be so easy to dispose of.

'This is a damned nuisance,' said Ryan. 'If we weren't so near to the stage, I might have thought about shooting those bastards without warning, just to make sure they didn't get in our way.'

'Them on the coach would hear the shots,' said Lopez. 'Would put them on their guard, no?'

'Yeah, that's about the strength of it. You're up to killing them, though, if they interfere in anywise?'

Lopez smiled. 'But of course. What's another three deaths between friends?'

They were now no more than two miles from the bright crimson Concorde which was thundering along the road towards them. And still they were behind the other riders, who would certainly, at this pace, reach the stage at exactly the same time as them.

The sight of an old red Concorde on the road was not as common as it had once been. Even in less-developed territories like this, most folk eschewed the stage in favour of the railroad. There was something grand about the sight of the horses pulling along that shiny red coach and even Ryan, who was the least sentimental of individuals, thought it something of a pity that one didn't see the stages as much as was once the case. Then there was no time for such nostalgic thoughts, because they were nigh on top of the stagecoach. It was then, at the very moment that Ryan would have taken oath, that he knew to the last detail how things would work out, that everything began to unravel.

The three men who were ahead of Ryan and Lopez did indeed reach the stagecoach almost at the same instant as they did themselves. Instead of forging past the coach and continuing along the road to Phoenix though, the other party of riders slowed down and then wheeled round in a wide arc, heading back along the road, behind the stage. This was precisely the manoeuver that Ryan had been aiming for, and for the merest fraction of a second, he was wholly unable to apprehend what it meant to see these others carrying out that movement. It was only for a moment or two though, because no sooner were the three riders galloping along behind the stagecoach, than they began shooting at the driver and the two fellows on the roof who were riding shotgun.

'Son of a bitch,' cried Ryan, 'Those whore's sons are after robbin' that stage as well!' Bullets were now whistling past him and Lopez, as the men coming up behind the stage unleashed a perfect hail of fire at the crew. The stage was almost upon them in any case, and Ryan and Lopez veered off the road and out of the path of the shooting. As soon as they were clear of the gunfire and the stagecoach had passed them by, the men turned their horses in a great circle and began galloping frantically after the coach themselves. It was then that all hell broke loose.

It was not possible to see if any of the men on the roof had been killed so far. At any rate, none had fallen from the stagecoach. What happened as Ryan and Lopez took up the pursuit was that the windows at the side facing them suddenly bristled with gun barrels, and they found themselves caught in withering and deadly accurate fire from at least three men with repeating rifles. Lopez was killed almost immediately, as was one of the three men who had initiated the assault on the stage. A bullet droned past Ryan's ear, sounding like an angry hornet.

Another of the riders went down and it struck Ryan most forcibly that unless he made tracks right this second, he was apt to be the next casualty. He changed direction and galloped off as fast as his horse could take him. The men in the coach kept firing and when he glanced back, Ryan saw that all the other riders were down and that the Concorde had halted.

As he headed back to Yuma, Ryan turned over in his mind the events which he had lately witnessed. Lopez was no special loss; he'd been hoping anyway to find some way of ridding himself of the Mexican. It was a shame about the gold he'd been carrying with him, though. When all was said and done, Ryan had about $3,500 with him right now in his saddle-bag. Then his face lit up with pleasure. He had twice that much! That fool Lopez left his own money in his room at The Supreme. He could surely outpace that stage in getting to Yuma. All that was needed was for him to race up to Lopez's room and collect the money hidden there. Then he would be on the road with maybe $7,000 all to himself. The thought of being alone and free, with such a sum of money all to himself gave Ryan a warm glow inside. He was safe and had come out ahead of the game, as he always did.

'Sorry if I'm a little slow on the uptake here, Birrell,' said Sheriff Nugent, 'You know what us small town folks are like. Not as sharp as some of you fellows from the big city. Let me go over this one last time.'

'It's easy enough . . .' began Birrell, before the sheriff cut in right sharp.

'Shut up, Birrell. I tell you straight, I've seen and heard about enough of you to last me the rest of my life. You came here to my town looking for those men as robbed the *Tucson Flyer*. You didn't have the professional courtesy to come by my office and let me know what was going on in my town. And now, three men have been killed. Have I got that right?'

'Couldn't have put it better myself,' said Birrell.

Nugent looked hard at the man from the railroad, as though he was trying to work out if Birrell was being too smart. Then he said, 'Now the two members of the gang, other than Tucker who you shot, have dug up and left town. And you say that you'd no idea that this Patrick McFadden was in town at all?'

'I didn't know he was here and I don't know how he's mixed up in this. The company sets one man on a job and then, odd times, puts another on the same trail without telling him. There's a deal of dishonesty in the world, sheriff. You wouldn't believe it. That way, one man keeps a watch on the other. Maybe McFadden was supposed to be watching me.'

'That what you think?'

'No, not really. I think it was coincidence.'

'Nice idea. Was it coincidence that led him to meet the same killer as accounted for Pete Owen? That same Pete Owen that you'd been threatening? No, there's more to this than meets the eye.'

'Be that as it may, am I free to go yet? I've still got

109

eight or nine thousand dollars' worth o' gold to track down.'

Nugent looked surprised at the suggestion. 'You're going nowhere for a while, Mr Birrell,' he said. 'Tell you what, it's coming up time to eat. Must be about one or later. We'll go and find a meal somewhere, you and me. But you stick right by my side 'til I give you leave to go. Understood?'

'I guess.'

It was after half one and Quincy was utterly sick of that little piece of the street that he had been pacing up and down along all the day long. There was no doubt at all now that people had marked him and were wondering what he was about. He had tried looking in the store windows, humming a little tune, looking up at the sky and just standing still in one spot, but whatever he did, it was obvious to everybody around that he was really watching the hotel. He stayed there much longer and somebody would be informing on him to the sheriff's office and he would be taken up as a loitering thief.

His stomach was rumbling and he had almost come to the decision that it would be all right to leave his post for a few minutes, when Quincy saw Ryan riding down the street towards him. He ducked under the awning of a nearby store before he was seen, and observed that Ryan looked even more dishevelled and disreputable than usual. He was alone as well and that in itself was curious. What had become of Lopez? Outside The Supreme, Ryan dismounted and twisted the reins around a post. It didn't look like he was fixing to stay long, wherever he was going. Then, having secured his horse in a cursory fashion, Ryan went into The Supreme. In a flash, Quincy was after him.

The young fellow behind the counter called to Quincy as he dashed past, but there was too much at stake to worry about upsetting some little clerk. Quincy sprinted up the stairs and peered down the first corridor he came to. It was empty. He ran up to the next floor and there, at the end of the corridor, he saw Ryan about to enter a room. 'Ryan,' he said loudly, 'I got a crow to pluck with you.'

Not in the slightest degree discomposed, Ryan turned to face him. 'Hey there, Quincy,' he said, 'I woulda thought you were dead by now. I'd like to chat, but I'm in a hurry right now. Some other time.' Then he turned away and made as though to enter the room.

'You make a move, Ryan and you're a dead man.'

Slowly and with great reluctance, Ryan turned back to face him. He said, 'Well then, what will you have? Make it quick.'

'You left me to die, Ryan. I'll let that ride for now. I'll take my share of that gold, though.'

'There's been a change in our share-out. We figured you wouldn't want yours anymore.'

It was then that Quincy knew that he hadn't needed to come up here and brace Ryan. Like as not, his share of the money was in the saddle-bag on his horse. 'I guess then I'll take your share,' he told the other man. 'It'll be on your horse this minute, is that right?'

Ryan stepped into the very middle of the corridor and faced Quincy squarely. He said, 'Time to end what I begun back in the Gila. You ready?'

'You'll see,' said Quincy tersely.

The sound of gunfire rocked the narrow corridor of the hotel, the three shots being so close together that they sounded like one deafening and sustained roar. Ryan didn't have any time at all to register shock or amazement at being bested by this slow-talking man. Quincy had put the first shot into his adversary's chest, which caused Ryan's own shot to go wide of the mark. The second bullet, Quincy aimed right between the other man's eyes. Ryan's heart had stopped beating before his body landed on the carpeted floor.

As he holstered the Remington, Quincy thought to himself that the action was smoother in practice than he had expected. It had, anyway, done the job and that was the only thing that really mattered. There was no point in standing there like a fool. In next to no time, the hotel would be swarming with men from the sheriff's office. As he made his way rapidly down the grand staircase, Quincy's mind was working feverishly. He didn't think that he had left anything at all that could identify him in the lodging house where he had been staying. Similarly, the saddle at the livery stable was a cheap, used item that he had picked up after he'd come out of the desert. He would sure hate to lose that tough little pony, but then again, he didn't much fancy fooling around and tacking up the animal while a posse was on his tail. There outside The Supreme was a good mount and unless he missed his guess, there was at least three or four thousand in the saddle-bag.

Thrusting his hand into the saddle-bag of Ryan's horse confirmed what Quincy had suspected and devoutly hoped; it was full of gold coins. All that was needful now was for him to make tracks as swiftly as ever he might to Maricopa Wells, and somehow get Geoffrey Hanigan's aunt to accept the ill-gotten gains on behalf of her nephew. That might be easier said than done, but he had to make the attempt. Quincy leapt into the saddle and rode off, heading for the road east out of Yuma.

Sheriff Nugent behaved during the meal with Birrell almost as though he was off duty. He had been very irritated at the railroad detective's cavalier approach, but there was probably no harm done. He pegged Birrell for a straight operator and Nugent always appreciated that in a man.

'Tell me, Mr Birrell, if I tie up my own inquiries fairly soon, what are your intentions?'

'That mean that you don't propose to put me on trial?'

Nugent laughed. 'You say you were a detective in the Chicago City Police. Tell me straight, what would you have done, had you found some private citizen mixed up in three murders? Specially where this fellow had been playing policeman in your district, without so much as a by-your-leave?'

'I would have booted his behind and maybe locked him up for a while.'

'Well, then. I don't think you got too much to complain of. I just hope the next time you come to Yuma, you at least drop by my office first and let me know what's going on.'

Birrell shrugged and said, 'I suppose I'm in the habit of playing a lone hand. You never know when the other party will behave sensibly, if once you let others get involved in your affairs.'

The two men understood each other well enough and both had measured the other against their own standards and were satisfied with the results. It was then that the door to the little eating house flew open and the deputy called Rob burst in, shouting, 'Sheriff, there's been shooting up at The Supreme Hotel. A man's been killed dead.'

The acrid smell of gunpowder in the hotel corridor was overpowering. Stretched lifeless on the floor was a man in his early thirties, at least by the look of him. There were two bullet wounds on his body; one in his chest and the other dead between his eyes.

'That's a neat piece of shooting,' said Birrell, 'Whoever killed this fellow wanted to make sure that he stayed dead.'

'You recognize him?' asked the sheriff.

'No, but I'll hazard a guess that this is one of the four men who robbed the *Tucson Flyer*.'

'What, the men you've been hunting?'

'Yeah. The descriptions fit him.'

'Him and a hundred others in town,' snorted Sheriff Nugent, 'Let me guess, the description is of a man with even features, no distinguishing marks, between five eight and six feet. Something like that?'

'Yes, well. Can we search him?'

'There's no "we" in the case, Mr Birrell. This is my town and I'll undertake the necessary investigations. I don't mind you tagging along at my side, but we'll do things my way. Understood?'

There was nothing in the dead man's pockets to say who he might have been in life. Staff at the hotel said that he had spent a night there and had left a deposit when he left that morning, on the understanding that he might be coming back to stay another night. There was a suspicion that they might have been the chief instigators of a brawl which had broken out last night in the bar-room downstairs.

'They're the boys, for a bet,' said Birrell, 'Can we look in their rooms?'

'Anybody been in their rooms since they left?' asked Sheriff Nugent, turning to the counter clerk.

'No, sir. That's why they paid a deposit, to keep the option on having the rooms again tonight.'

'All right, let's have a look. See if they left anything worth seeing in there.'

Ryan's room yielded nothing, but tucked carelessly under the pillow on the bed in Lopez's room was a canvas bag containing over $3,000 in gold.

'I reckon that clinches it,' said Birrell, 'I'll take this over to the bank.'

'Not yet, you won't,' said Nugent, 'There's a little more to be found out.'

After more questioning of different employees of

The Supreme, it was established that a man of about
forty had run into the hotel, shortly before the
shooting and then ran out again afterwards. The
clerk said to Birrell, 'He was standing right behind
you this very morning, sir.'

'How's that?' asked the detective, startled.

'You recollect that you came by here this
morning, asking about a white man and a Mexican
who might have been staying here?'

'Yes, yes,' said Birrell, 'Of course I remember. It
was only a few hours ago. What of it?'

'Well, there was a fellow standing right behind
you when you was asking me those questions.'

Sheriff Nugent said, 'You say this person was the
one who ran in and then ran off again round about
the time that this man was shot?'

'Yes sir, that's right.'

'What about it, Birrell?' the sheriff asked him.
'Think you'd know him again?'

'No, I hardly looked at him. There's something
funny going on here.'

'You got a different idea of what's funny,' said
Nugent dryly. 'That's the fourth violent death now
and all of them connected with you. Who would you
say this man was that was behind you in line this
morning?'

Augustus Birrell shook his head. Fact was, he
wasn't overly concerned about the matter. He had
recovered over half the money that had been stolen
from the train and from all that he was able to
collect, two of the men who had taken part in the

crime were now dead. Things were shaping up very nicely. It was then that one of Nugent's other deputies turned up, with the news that a stage lately arrived in town had been ambushed on the road from Phoenix and that four bandits had been killed in the attack, as well as one of the men riding shotgun on the stage.

Sheriff Nugent said to Birrell, 'I don't suppose that this latest news has anything to do with you, Mr Birrell? You seem to be associated with most of the deaths lately, you sure these aren't friends of yours as well?'

'I cannot conceive how the ambush-robbery of a stagecoach could be connected with the men I've been searching for.'

'You want to come with me and see what it's all about?'

'Don't see why not.'

Quincy had no idea how long it would be before anybody set out in pursuit of him. He certainly had to put as much distance between himself and Yuma as he could possibly manage. The only thing was, Ryan's horse didn't seem too lively. Quincy had the impression that the horse had already put in quite a bit of work already today.

All things considered, Quincy was satisfied with the way that everything had panned out. He'd revenged himself upon the man he was sure had been the main driving force behind the decision to leave him helpless and defenceless in the middle of the Gila Desert. Not only that, he had secured the money that he felt was owed to him. There was no time right now to stop and count it, but a quick glance had been enough to assure him that there must be at least $3,000 in that saddle-bag.

How would he be able to get Geoffrey Hanigan's aunt to take this large sum of money from a complete stranger? This was something of a poser and Quincy had no idea how he would be able to work that one. Still and all, that could wait. The main thing now was to get the cash to Maricopa Wells and then play it from there.

On his travels south to Arizona, Quincy seemed to remember some talk about trouble with the Apache in this part of the territory. Had they been raiding across the border from Mexico or something? It would be right funny if having steered his course so skillfully up to now, he fell at the last fence and ended up being scalped by a bunch of Redskins! He laughed out loud at the thought.

Ryan's horse really wasn't in a brilliant condition for a long ride such as Quincy had in mind. Lord knows how far its owner had already ridden it today, but every time he eased up on the spurs, the creature relapsed into a plodding walk. He looked back anxiously, fearing to see signs of pursuit. He surely would not be able to outrun a posse on this beast. Maybe he would have done better to take the time to tack up that Indian pony and bring that instead. At least it had had a good night's rest and would have been fresh for this journey. Well, there was nothing to be done about it. He'd just have to make the best of things. Sometimes you had to play the hand you were dealt and not the one you would have chosen for yourself.

CHAPTER 9

Augustus Birrell had been biding his time with the sheriff and waiting for a chance to slip away. He figured that he and Nugent were on warm enough terms now that the man wouldn't be watching him every second. After all, this new attempted robbery alone was enough to occupy Sheriff Nugent and his deputies to the limit of their powers for the rest of the day. He didn't wish to make a big production out of leaving, though. He gave every appearance of being relaxed and in no sort of hurry to move on anywhere else.

The main point exercising Birrell's mind was that the man shot to death in The Supreme had left his horse tethered outside and the man who had probably killed him had immediately jumped on his victim's horse and ridden off. Why had he done so? The obvious answer, leastways to the wily detective, was that some of the gold from the train robbery was slung over the saddle of that beast. In the Mexican's hotel room, three and a half thousand had been found; presumably his share of the proceeds. Where was the other man's then, he that had been killed? Obviously, he was carrying it on his horse. If for no other reason than this, then, Birrell was determined to go after this man. There was more, though. Who actually was the fellow? He had been standing right behind Birrell at The Supreme. What was his interest in the business? And why had he killed one of the men who was most likely responsible for the attack on the *Tucson Flyer*?

When Birrell put the question like that, he saw the answer at once. Who would want to kill one of the men responsible for carrying out the robbery on the train? He'd already worked out that three of the gang had, somewhere along the way, ditched one of their number. That was why he had only been able to find evidence of three of the four men who had undertaken the robbery, here in Yuma. It also explained the fact that the man he'd shot had been carrying more than $3,000. The same applied to the share that the Mexican had in his hotel room, of course.

Assuming that one member of the gang had been disposed of, everything fitted neatly into place.

What if he'd been wrong in taking it for granted that such men would have simply killed the man they wished to cheat out of his share? Birrell ran that round a bit and it too seemed to fit perfectly and explain an awful lot that was otherwise mysterious and inexplicable. The cheated man had come here, seeking vengeance against those who had betrayed him. Now he'd taken back the gold that he saw as being rightfully his.

All this had been figured out while Birrell was talking to Sheriff Nugent and walking around Yuma with him. So busy was Nugent with arranging for men to go out and retrieve the bodies of the bandits who'd attacked the stage and sundry other matters, that he couldn't later recall when last he saw the railroad detective. Birrell had been at his side and moving about nearby, examining evidence and suchlike and then later on, he was not. Well, when all was said and done, it was no big deal. As a matter of fact, it might make Nugent's work easier when it came to compiling his report. He would be able to edit out Birrell and present the whole investigation in the correct light, with him, Nugent, as the man of the hour.

The only unknown for Birrell had been which way the escaping man had fled from Yuma. There was nothing to choose really between any direction. This was where the years that he had spent in the regular police came in handy. This fellow was a smart one. He must figure that somebody would chase after him, having after all committed a murder in the best hotel in town like that. Which would be the best way to head, if you wished to put folk off your trail? The answer to that was glaringly obvious. If the fellow really had been part of the gang that robbed the train, then the last place anybody would be expecting him to head for was of course Maricopa Wells. Once his horse was saddled up, it was accordingly east that Augustus Birrell headed, as fast as his horse would carry him.

He had been fearing, and half expecting, a posse. When he looked back for the hundredth time though, all that Quincy could make out was one, lone rider, following along behind him. If Ryan's horses had been in any fit state, then he would have set it at a gallop and done his damnedest to outrun the man behind him. But the horse he was riding was plumb tuckered out and it was taking all Quincy's efforts to keep the beast moving at a trot; never mind breaking into a gallop. Beside which, there was nothing to say that the rider coming up behind him was really pursuing him. It might be just some random traveller, who chanced to be heading in the same direction as Quincy himself.

Well, thought Quincy, after he had urged on the horse and been rewarded by its stopping dead in the road for a minute, before plodding on at a walk, let what will be, be. There's little enough I can do about it. He toyed briefly with the idea of waiting until the other rider caught up and then shooting him without offering any challenge, but his sense of fair play revolted at the very thought of such a scheme. He would scorn to kill a fellow being at unawares. No, he would need to face what came.

So it was that an hour later, Augustus Birrell caught up with Quincy and hailed him in a friendly enough fashion, saying, 'Well met, friend. You and me seem to be heading the same way. What say we ride together for a while?'

Quincy shrugged. 'Tell you the truth, and I don't mean to offend you or nothin', I'm fond enough o' my own company. Still and all, if you want a companion for a spell, let's carry on together. The choice is yours.'

Short of telling the stranger to get to hell and leave him alone, Quincy could hardly have made his feelings more plain. But Birrell hadn't risen through the ranks of the Chicago police by being specially thin-skinned and delicate. He noted that his presence was unwelcome to the other man and just brought his mount alongside the other horse, like he had been greeted as a welcome fellow traveller.

Neither of the men spoke for a while. Birrell was racking his brains and trying to remember if he had ever seen this man before. It would be the devil of a business, were he to draw his gun and challenge this quiet man and then find out that he was nothing to do with the robbery at Maricopa Wells or any of the trouble in Yuma. He decided to play it by ear for a while and see if he could draw out the other man. For his part, Quincy too was in doubt. He recognized this as the man who had stood in front of him at The Supreme, but was he a lawman or what? So the two of them rode on; each gripped by doubt about the other.

At length, Birrell broke the uncomfortable silence, saying, 'This is a lonely road. Are you heading for Maricopa Wells or some nearer place?'

'I'm aiming to ride east,' was all that Quincy

would say, 'What about yourself?'

'I reckon I'm going east as well.'

There was silence again for ten minutes or so and then Birrell said, 'You come from Yuma, perhaps?'

'It could be so,' replied Quincy, noncommittally, 'You?'

'Yes,' said Birrell, 'I've come from there.'

Lord, thought Birrell, this is like drawing teeth. If only I could sneak a look in that saddle-bag of his, I could settle the matter in a moment. I could draw down on him and then take him back to Yuma. But I surely don't want to be pointing a gun at some innocent man. If nothing else, it would be right embarrassing, to say nothing of risking my own life for nought. So he did nothing, but after a quarter hour, remarked, 'They say that lone travellers are at hazard hereabouts. The Apache are restless. I do hear that the army might be forced to lend a hand.'

'Is that a fact?'

'Yes, there's been folk killed. Out in lonely farms and such, you know.'

'Is that a wagon ahead of us? There, maybe three miles down the trail. Anyways, it's a piece of white. Something of the sort, I'd say.'

'A wagon?' replied Birrell, 'Surely not. Those days are gone. I doubt you'd find any emigrants heading to Yuma in a Prairy Schooner.' He laughed at the thought.

Quincy reined in and said, 'Look yonder. The heat shimmers make it uncertain, but there, nigh on the horizon. Can you see a glimmer of white?'

Birrell stared hard in the direction that the other man was indicating. 'I could do with a pair of field glasses,' he muttered, 'But yes, there's something there. What puts you in mind of wagons?'

'What else d'you think it's like to be? The sail of a boat?'

The two men rode on at a steady pace, their senses alert to anything unusual in the bleak landscape around them. The plain across which they were riding was as flat as a flannel cake and they could see for at least three or four miles in every direction. Nothing stirred.

After a while, Birrell said, 'Lord strike me dead if I don't reckon as you're right. I think that is a covered wagon. Although what it might be doing in these parts is anybody's guess.'

By the time that they were a mile and a half away, it was perfectly obvious that a wagon lay ahead of them on the road. Or rather just off the road. There was no sign of a horse and as they drew nearer, they could see that the contents of the wagon had been strewn across the ground; as though somebody had been searching for something and angrily discarded everything in which he was not interested.

When they were a couple of hundred yards from the wagon, Birrell said, 'Hold up now, my friend. Let's stop here a minute.'

'Why, what's to do?'

'Angle that thing's slewed across the way, we can't see inside it from here.'

'So?'

'So what if somebody, or more than one person, is sitting inside there with repeating rifles and getting ready to fire on us as we ride up?'

The thought hadn't crossed Quincy's mind. He said, 'Why would anybody do such a thing?'

'I don't rightly know. Why would anybody ransack a covered wagon and then leave it by the roadside in that way? It's an odd business, whichever way you approach it.'

Quincy rubbed his jaw thoughtfully. Then he said, 'Why don't we split up and one of us go from one way and the other, another. We both got pistols. Why don't we cock our pieces and be ready for trouble?'

'Was going to make the self-same suggestion myself. Great minds think alike, or so they say. You want to take left or right?'

'Left.'

As he drew closer to the wagon, Quincy thought that he could see a body lying on the ground, right by the great spiked wheels. He peered hard to try and make sure, and it was while he was doing so that he caught the flash of movement inside the wagon itself. The stranger had been right; there was somebody hiding inside. He reined in and then drew down on the canvas hood. There was no other sign of life, so he urged on the horse at a slow walk; never once taking his eyes off the wagon.

Birrell too was taking no chances. He moved in slowly from the other side; pistol in hand and ready to fire at the least provocation. Quincy had the impression that they were like two cautious hunters, trying to corner a dangerous animal. When he was just twenty-five yards from the wagon, Quincy slipped off his horse and then loped the rest of the way, the Remington cocked and ready. When he reached the side of the canvas hood safely, he paused for a second and then darted to the flap covering the back of the wagon and jerked it suddenly aside, his pistol aimed at the interior. A child began screaming in terror.

CHAPTER 10

His name was Bobby and he was six years old. The man lying dead with a half dozen arrows in him was his father. Bobby had been travelling to Yuma in this wagon with his ma and pa, but they had been ambushed by Indians. His ma had been taken by them, but they'd shown no interest in him. After looting the wagon and taking some stuff, he didn't know what, the Redskins had ridden off and left him here. He'd crawled into the wagon and hidden. When this had happened, Bobby couldn't rightly say, but it seemed to have been earlier that same day.

'Which means,' said Birrell in a low voice, when he and Quincy were talking a little way from the boy, 'That like as not, those who did this are still in the area.'

'It's a hell of a thing for a child that age to go through,' said Quincy, looking compassionately at the grief-stricken boy. 'Why d'you think that someone took his ma but left him?'

'Maybe so's they could rape her. Could be ransom

or, if she's young enough, they'll maybe trade her to some brothel south of the border. I don't know.'

'God almighty,' said Quincy, shaking his head, 'What a dreadful thing to befall a little boy.'

'Well, there's little enough we can do about it . . .' began Birrell.

'Well, we sure as hell can't leave him here!' said Quincy indignantly. His raised voice caused the child to look up, wondering if more violence was about to disrupt his life.

Quincy lowered his voice and said, 'Look, mister, happen it's time for some plain dealing.'

'The name's Birrell, Augustus Birrell.'

'Quincy. I've a notion that you meeting me on the road wasn't chance at all. I'd say you think you got business to settle with me. I'll be happy to accommodate you, if that's the way of it. But not now. We've got to get that poor helpless child to safety before we look at what lies between the two of us.'

Birrell didn't say anything for a time. He looked into Quincy's face and saw a man who wouldn't play him false. They might well end up with one of them killing the other, but this Quincy was not a treacherous type. He said, 'You mean, Mr Quincy, that we shelve our differences until this boy is cared for and then see what's what?'

'That's the way of it. What d'you say?'

Birrell put out his hand and said, 'I say, you got a deal.' Quincy reached out his hand and the two men shook, each of them liking the look of the other and being well assured that there would be no trickery or oath-breaking.

'Well,' Birrell said, 'How do you propose we make a beginning, Mr Quincy?'

'That young'un can't ride in front of us on our saddles for all those miles to Maricopa Wells. The Indians took the horse, but there's no reason we can't harness one of ours up to the wagon.'

'I reckon that would be a smart move. You mean one of us ride with the boy in the wagon and the other riding?'

'Yes, that's how I see the best way to proceed.'

The arrangement required a good deal of trust on the part of both men. What, thought Birrell, if I end up in the wagon, with a horse all hitched up and that Quincy riding alongside. What's to stop him from galloping off and leaving me to take care for the child? By the time I unharnessed the other horse and got saddled up, he could be miles away. Even if I did feel able to abandon the boy out here in the wild.

For his part, Quincy had a separate set of anxieties about the business. They would have to camp somewhere for at least one night. Suppose this Birrell were to disarm him while he was asleep and then make him prisoner? It was taking much on trust. Still, in cases such as this, a man must trust his instincts and whatever else he was, Augustus Birrell looked straight as they come. Quincy would have to take a chance on it.

While the two of them were tacking up Birrell's horse to draw the wagon, its owner had a thought.

He wondered if he'd been buffaloed into a false path.

'Say, he said, 'What's to hinder us going back to Yuma, rather than going on to Maricopa Wells?' Birrell could not help be suspicious, now that he considered the matter carefully. If Quincy was that bothered about this child's welfare, why hadn't he suggested that they race back to Yuma with the boy?

'Step aside with me for a second, Mr Birrell,' said Quincy. 'Bobby boy, you set here and rest. Don't be afeared o' nothing. Me and this gentleman are going to get you safe out of this, don't you fret none.'

When he and Birrell were out of earshot of the child, Quincy said in a soft voice, 'How good are your eyes, Mr Birrell?'

'Fair to middling. I can see most clearly close up. Why?'

'Turn your gaze upon those low hills, right across west, between us and Yuma.'

'What am I supposed to be looking at?'

'Can you see aught on the slopes? Look like little black dots.'

'Your eyes are better than mine, but I can almost make out something. What is it?'

'It's people moving about. There were none such when I rode past those hills a few hours back.'

'You think it's Apaches?'

'Maybe. You want to take a chance by riding back that way? Recollect, we have that little'un to think of, no matter how brave we're feeling.'

'Maricopa Wells it is then. Think those boys can see us from where they are?'

'If I can make out single men, then I reckon they'll be able to see a moving wagon with a white hood on it like this one.'

There was nothing more to be said, so once the harness was all in order, the little party set off along the road to Maricopa Wells.

To begin with, Quincy drove the wagon, with the boy sitting next to him, while Birrell rode alongside on Ryan's horse. Quincy said to the child, when once they were under way, 'Tell me about yourself, Bobby.' The boy looked at him blankly and Quincy realized that he might be a little young for such a broad and sweeping question. He tried to be a little more specific.

'Why were you folks going to Yuma?'

'My pa said we was going to live on a farm.'

'A farm, hey? Any notion where this farm might have been?'

'No, sir, my pa, he said as it was near Mexico.'

'Was it a homesteading enterprise?'

The boy's face brightened and he said, 'Yes, that was the word my pa used. Homestead.'

'You got any folks that you stayed with before you set out? Exceptin' your ma and pa, that is.'

The boy thought about this question for a while and then said, 'We lived near Tucson. I never seed any aunts nor uncles. Nothin' o' that sort. Only kin I had was my ma and pa.' Upon which, the poor little mite began weeping; a hopeless and inconsolable

133

sobbing that Quincy had no idea how to cope with. Birrell caught his eye and shook his head, as though to say, 'What can we do?'

Birrell was having no better luck with Ryan's horse than Quincy had had. It plodded on, stopping dead from time to time and resisting all efforts on the part of the rider to get it moving again. After the twentieth such halt, Birrell said, 'Where the Dickens did you get this nag? It's dead on its feet.'

'That's by way of being a long story.'

'Yes, I'll be bound it is,' said Birrell, shooting the man on the wagon a meaningful look.

CHAPTER 11

By dusk, Ryan's horse would go no further. Gradually, it had refused to move at anything more than a trot and then, by degrees, had relapsed into a walk. After another two hours, it was taking all Augustus Birrell's efforts to persuade it even to walk.

'It's no manner of use digging your spurs in anymore,' said Quincy, 'The poor beast is just about done to death. If we're hoping to travel on in the same way tomorrow, we'd best let it get some rest now. What say we camp up for the night?'

The figures that they had seen on the hills which lay between them and Yuma had vanished from sight, and since there was no sign of pursuit, Birrell and Quincy were optimistic that they might not be molested during the hours of darkness.

As they unharnessed the wagon, Birrell said, 'I wonder if we wouldn't be better advised to strike north and try to intercept the railroad line. We could flag down the next train and be safe.'

Quincy gave the other man a curious look. 'You

don't reckon that any of the Southern Pacific trains as see men trying to halt 'em, might not find it better policy to speed up, rather than slowin' down?'

'You refer to the late robberies, I guess?'

'That's right.'

While they were preparing some sort of evening meal, from the food supplies which they had found in the wagon, Birrell found himself separated from Quincy and near the horse that Quincy and he had been riding that day. He was smitten with a sudden desire to settle the question one way or another, by simply opening the saddle-bag and looking inside. Would he find $3,000 or so in gold? If so, then he would know at once that his suspicions were on the money and that the man he was riding with now had been a member of the gang which hit the *Tucson Flyer*. The impulse passed, swiftly enough. After all, they had shaken hands on a deal and suspended any possible hostility between themselves until they had got the little boy to safety. What sort of skunk would he be making of himself, if he started sneaking and skulking in breach of this agreement?

Young Bobby's parents had certainly made good provisions for their journey to wherever it was they were heading. The Indians had taken anything else worth stealing, but they'd seemingly had no use for the foodstuffs and kegs of water. The two men and the boy feasted that night on a broiled fowl, and also various vegetables they boiled up over the campfire, which Bobby said his father had brought down.

'You think it wise, starting up a fire with those

Redskins on the prowl?' asked Birrell, when they were away from the boy and gathering wood for the fire.

Quincy grunted. 'If those boys are still around, they'll know all about us already. Makes no odds if we have a fire or not. 'Sides which, the child looks as though he needs warming up and feeding.'

They both made great efforts to cheer up the little boy and draw him out of himself as they sat and ate. At first, the child responded with monosyllables, but he gradually became livelier, although always with that desolate look upon his face.

'So tell us 'bout your life, Bobby, before you and your folks took to the road,' said Quincy, 'Must've been quite an adventure for you to leave your home like this.'

'Pa had trouble with getting work. He wanted to be a farmer, 'stead o' working for somebody else.'

'Well,' said Birrell, 'I can't find it in my heart to blame him. I ain't exactly over-fond of working for other people myself.'

Quincy looked at the other man over the fire and said, 'I'm surprised at that. Have you ever set up business on your own account?'

'Not yet,' said Birrell, 'But I'm going to have a little concern of my own. You wait.'

Quincy skillfully drew the boy into the chaffing, by saying to him, 'Ask him what he has in mind, Bobby. Go on. See what sort of a business he's goin' to run.'

Bobby said timidly, 'What will you be doin', sir?'

'I'll tell you, my boy. I'm fixing to have my own

detective agency, one to rival Pinkertons. There now, what d'you say to that?'

The boy's eyes shone in the flickering firelight. 'Gee, that sounds fine.'

It was on the very tip of Quincy's tongue to make some mocking remark, but then he saw the expression on Bobby's face and clamped his mouth firmly shut. After all, if this conversation was taking the child's mind away from his grief, then that was good. Bobby looked over to him and said, 'What do you do, sir?'

'Yes,' said Birrell, a mischievous twinkle in his eye, 'I was wondering much the same thing myself. Come now, Mr Quincy, what *do* you do for a living?'

Ignoring Birrell, Quincy turned to the boy and said gravely, 'Well, now young Bobby, I do a bit of this and a bit of that.'

'That's vague enough,' said Birrell. 'What do you mean by it?'

Still looking at the child's face, Quincy said, 'It's plain enough. Today, I'm doing a bit of this and then tomorrow, why, I'll be doing a bit of that.' He was rewarded by seeing Bobby smile. Well, he thought to himself, if I've made the boy laugh, then I haven't wasted my time.

The two men continued in this way, scoring points off each other and amusing the young boy in the process. After an hour or so of this sort of conversation, Quincy noticed that Bobby's eyelids were drooping and that the child was all but asleep. He stood up and then gathered the slight body in his arms. 'It's all right,' he whispered, 'You've nothing to fear.' The child's eyes closed again. Quincy put him in the wagon and wrapped him in a blanket. Then he went back to the fire.

'You want some more coffee?' asked Birrell. 'There's no shortage of the stuff, so I reckon we might just as well drink our fill.'

They sat there for a while, sipping their coffee and staring into the flames. Quincy said quietly, 'It's decent of you to agree about putting aside our differences until that lad is safe. I appreciate it.'

'It's all we can do. We're both men, I suppose. What would we be if we started fighting and wrestling with each other and left that child to fend for himself. He was smiling a little, at least that's something.'

'Now that he can't hear us, there's something else needs saying. I've heard stories about the Apaches being on the warpath and I dare say you heard the same. Goin' by what happened to his ma and pa, I'd say as this country round here ain't precisely safe.'

Birrell reached over and stirred up the fire, illuminating his face in a blaze of light. 'Then what?' he asked. 'What do you say we should do?'

'There's little enough we *can* do. I was only meaning that we must take care tomorrow. I'll warrant that we'll come across some band of those devils somewhere between here and Maricopa Wells.'

'You done any Indian fighting?'

'A little. I was a scout for some years. I know

139

enough of the game to know that if we meet a large band, we're done for. If it's one or two, or even a half dozen, we might get free of the toils. I wouldn't like to put money on it though.'

'You're a regular Jeremiah,' grumbled Birrell, 'The Indian wars are over. Those Apache are little more than bandits.'

Quincy shrugged. 'Even bandits can kill people. If we end up with arrows in our backs, it'll be little comfort to tell ourselves that we were victims of banditry and not casualties of war.'

Augustus Birrell said nothing for a space, but stared moodily into the fire. Then he said, 'I hope we don't have any trouble, for the boy's sake. I'm thinking that men like you and me can handle murder and mayhem a sight better than a little thing like that.'

'Yeah, we'll just have to do our best. I'm goin' to turn in now, what about you?'

'Yes, me too. You think we should start early in the morning?'

'The earlier, the better.'

The day dawned sunny and bright. Quincy woke first, not long after the sun rose and he built a fire, so that they might have a pot of coffee before starting off. When the flames were leaping up around the pot, he woke Birrell. Neither of them wanted to disturb Bobby's slumbers, both realizing, without saying as much out loud, that while the boy was asleep, he wasn't racked with grief for his dead parents. He woke soon enough though, of his own accord.

140

All three of them were cold and stiff. There was a good deal of stamping of feet and slapping arms around bodies, in order to try and warm up a little. There was still no shortage of food, even if the bread and cheese upon which they broke their fast could have been a little fresher. As they munched their food and swigged coffee, Quincy said to Birrell, 'You know this area better than us, maybe. How long d'you reckon it'll take to reach Maricopa Wells in this wagon?'

'We won't get there tonight,' said Birrell, 'With luck, we could make it by tomorrow afternoon. Bar the axle don't bust or anything.'

'Lord, don't say that,' said Quincy irritably, 'You'll set the evil eye on our journey.'

'I never had you pegged for the superstitious type, Mr Quincy,' Birrell said, in a teasing voice, 'Thought you were the more practical kind.'

After breakfast, they poured the dregs of the coffee on to the fire to extinguish it, and then harnessed up the wagon again. This time, they put Ryan's horse in the shafts and Quincy rode Birrell's horse, while its owner sat in the driving seat of the wagon, next to Bobby.

The land through which they were passing was fairly smooth, but with gentle inclines, too low to be called hills, undulating on either side of them. This meant that it wasn't possible for most of the time to see all that far ahead. From time to time, they would mount a rise and catch a glimpse of the land ahead. They had been proceeding peacefully for two hours or so, when Birrell signalled for Quincy to come nigh to the wagon and exchange a few words with him. When the man riding his horse was close enough, Birrell said, 'How do you read the situation?'

'Everything seems quiet enough, but I wouldn't mind getting on to some higher ground and seeing if I can see any distance. Might see if we are as alone as we seem to be.'

'You want to ride off a bit, scout out our trail for us?'

'Yeah, but I don't like to leave the boy too far behind. I want to be able to set a watch upon him.'

This sentiment was more than a little annoying to the railroad detective, who said sharply, 'You don't think that I can guard the boy as well as you?'

'Don't take on. I know what I can and can't do, but I don't know nothin' about you. I ain't saying as you're no good, don't think that for a moment.'

Slightly mollified, Birrell said, 'Just ride out and see what you can see. I'll take care of young Bobby here. Ain't that the case, son?'

'Yes, sir. I guess so.'

'All right,' said Quincy, not wishing to appear ungracious, 'I'll take a quick peep over yonder and see what's to be seen.' He spurred on Birrell's horse and rode ahead, up a rise of land that sloped upwards for more than a mile, blocking any view of the road beyond the ridge.

It was a mercy that Quincy had some experience of scouting, because otherwise his riding out ahead of the wagon might have precipitated the very disaster that he was so keen to avert. In the event, his cautious ways saved the day. Before he was at the top of the slope of land, Quincy dismounted and left the horse to graze a little. He hoped that the creature was used to the ways of the trail and would not wander off too far. He continued on foot, all the time keeping his eyes peeled and gauging how far it would be before he was at the top of the rise of land and able to view the road ahead. Of course, if he could see the road ahead, then a natural consequence would be that anybody on that road might very well see *him,* so for the last few yards, he dropped to his hands and knees and covered the last few yards in that way.

It was just as well that Quincy had taken the precaution of crawling to the top of the ridge, in order not to allow himself to be outlined against the sky. About a mile ahead of him were a group of men, standing around near a bunch of horses. He counted five men and a similar number of mounts. He couldn't tell much about the men from that distance, other than that they were Indians. He could make out lances and brightly-coloured cloth. The men didn't look to Quincy to be setting an ambush or anything, they were just standing there talking.

Very slowly, so that there was no sudden flash of movement to attract attention, Quincy crawled back down the slope, mounted the horse and left at a trot. He would have felt easier in his mind if he'd gone on at a walk; Indians were famously sensitive to the drumming of a horse's hoofs, which they could pick up through the vibrations in the ground, even when the rider himself was out of sight. He had to balance this risk against the urgent need to get back to the wagon and warn Birrell that it was not safe to proceed onwards. There was also a sharp fear in Quincy's mind that the men might have mounted already and be heading towards them.

Quincy wasted no time in setting out the situation to Birrell. Bobby, who was sitting next to the detective, looked terrified out of his wits at hearing about the Indians ahead, but there was no time to dissemble. Quincy was a sight more concerned with saving the boy's life, than he was with sparing his feelings.

'Well,' said Birrell, 'You're the scout and famous Indian fighter. What do you recommend?'

'We can't go forward, at least not yet awhiles. There's no point in going back, this wagon won't be able to outrun mounted men and then again, we can't take the wagon off the track. Running it over rough ground would be inviting an axle to snap.'

'So what d'you suggest?'

'We set here and wait.'

Both men checked their pistols and ensured that they had spare ammunition ready to hand. Neither Quincy nor Birrell could think of anything reassuring to say to the frightened boy, so they left him alone. It would be enough if they were able to save his life and get him in one piece to Maricopa Wells.

When the attack did come, it was almost an anticlimax. Neither the boy nor the two men were at all

144

surprised to see five riders appear on the ridge in front of the wagon. At first, the horsemen did nothing at all; just stayed up there on the higher ground, watching them and biding their time. Then they trotted down towards the wagon. 'Do you think they mean mischief?' asked Birrell.

'I don't aim to wait and find out,' replied Quincy, 'If they come close to us, I'll give them one warning shot above their heads and then it's shoot to kill.'

'I wish we had a rifle,' said Birrell fretfully, 'This sawn-off weapon of mine is grand for close quarters, but no use at a distance.'

'Lucky that I've got a proper gun that ain't been monkeyed around with, then,' was all that Quincy said. He turned to Bobby and said, 'Listen, son, you get in the back of the wagon there and lie down flat. You understand me? Don't come out nor even poke your head up, unless me or Mr Birrell here give you leave.' Quincy dismounted and tethered the horse to the back of the wagon.

The riders came on at an angle, obviously not wishing to approach the wagon head on. This in itself roused Quincy's suspicions, because generally speaking, peaceful Indians just rode up and greeted you; maybe proposed a little bartering. No, these boys were up to no good, but wanted to see how fierce the fight was going to be before they lit in and killed those in the wagon. That's fine and dandy, thought Quincy to himself. Just let them come closer than thirty yards and they'll soon see how things stand.

When they were fifty yards from the wagon, the five Indians began cantering straight at them, splitting off into one group of three and another of two. Three men were veering to the left and the other pair of riders to the right. There was, thought Quincy, no point at all in wasting a bullet in firing a warning shot. These fellows were making their intentions perfectly plain. He drew down on one of the men and fired. He was wide of the mark and immediately loosed off a second shot. This time, he had the satisfaction of seeing one of the men fall from his horse.

One of the things which struck Quincy as odd after the skirmish, was that none of the Indians had apparently been carrying a firearm. They seemed to be armed only with bows and light, springy lances. Mind, at close quarters, these things were every bit as effective as guns, as was amply demonstrated later in the encounter. As one of the men rode past, Quincy fired, but missed. Then the Indian turned as he passed and hurled his lance. If Quincy had been just a mite less agile himself, he would have been skewered to the side of the wagon. As it was, the point of the weapon tore his sleeve before it thudded into the wood. His reaction was swift and deadly; he fired at the back of the Indian who had thrown the lance, hitting him right between his shoulder blades.

Quincy could hear Birrell firing, away to his left, but didn't wish to take his eyes off the men he was himself dealing with. He just hoped that the other man knew his business. All the riders had now passed the wagon and Quincy risked a quick glance to his left. Birrell seemed to be all right, but that short-barreled weapon of his had proved singularly ineffective for this kind of work. Quincy had managed to kill two of the men bearing down on him, but Birrell hadn't accounted for any of them. There were still three riders wheeling round and preparing to come at them once again.

Quincy reloaded, his fingers working automatically, while he kept his eyes fixed on their adversaries. We might yet make it, he thought triumphantly. Always assuming that those boys don't have any friends in the neighbourhood who are likely to hear the shooting and come and lend a hand. Then there was no time for further thinking, because the remaining three Indians came at them at the gallop. Quincy fired twice, not hitting any of them and he heard Birrell firing.

Then there came one of those strange lulls that you get sometimes in the heat of battle, when, for a moment, everything falls quiet and you can even hear birds singing nearby, providing they haven't been scared off by the noise of battle. In that sudden, eerie silence, Quincy heard a noise that put him strongly in mind of a woodpecker hammering a tree. The only odd part was that this was not the repeated, rhythmic drumming of a woodpecker, but rather a single 'thwack', which had that distinctive hollow, reverberating note that a woodpecker's hammering gives. Then the noise returned, as Quincy shot down one of the three remaining men. An

arrow sheared through the canvas hood of the
wagon, making a ripping noise and then Quincy
fired again, taking another of the men in his back as
he rode past. It was enough and the surviving
member of the band galloped off at speed, leaving
the white men as victors.

Quincy could hardly believe it. They had
managed to best odds of more than two to one and
neither of them were even wounded. He went over
to congratulate Birrell, and perhaps at the same time
make a few teasing remarks about the uselessness
and folly of sawing off the barrels of perfectly good
weapons, thus rendering them ineffective when the
fighting got hot. Lord, there was nothing quite like
the sensation of having been in a fight like that and
having come through it in one piece. Quincy felt
right braced with life. Then he saw Birrell and in an
instant realized the significance of that loud thud,
like a woodpecker's hammer.

The arrow had taken Birrell somewhere beneath
his left shoulder, at the top of his chest. The
wounded man was sitting on the ground and if it
weren't for that arrow protruding from him, you
might have thought that he was just snatching a little
rest before they started off again. He didn't look to
be in pain, merely a weary state.

'Don't you move,' said Quincy. 'I know how to
deal with this sort of thing. It might hurt a little, but
you don't strike me as the cry-baby type.'

'You leave it be, Mr Quincy. You're no sort of
doctor and even if you were, there's nought as can

be done. It's gone clean through my lung there.'
Birrell spoke in short bursts, like a man who has
been running and needs to catch his breath.

'Don't say so,' said Quincy, horrified at this turn of
events, 'Why, we'll have you as right as a trivet in no
time.'

Birrell coughed and grimaced with the pain. A
little bright crimson blood escaped from his lips. Just
from the look of that vivid colour, Quincy could tell
immediately that Birrell was right. This was arterial
blood, straight from the lungs. He crouched down
and said, 'Can I do anything to help?'

'Hell, no!' said Birrell jovially. 'Think I don't know
when I'm done for?'

There didn't seem much more to be said. The
arrow had sliced straight into a lung and it was also
right close to the heart from the look of it. No doubt
Birrell was leaking blood into his chest cavity, this
very minute. 'You want that I should put a blanket
over you or some such?' Quincy asked.

'That'd be a kindness.'

Clambering up into the wagon, Quincy found
Bobby, who was still cowering in fear. He said to him,
'Bobby, you can come down now. There's nothing
more to be afeared of. Only thing is, Mr Birrell isn't
in too good a state. You might not want to see, so if'n
you'd sooner stop here, just say.'

'I'd like to get out, please, sir.'

'All right. Just hand me that blanket there, will
you?'

The two of them got down from the wagon, and as

soon as they were on the ground, the boy slipped his hand into Quincy's. It was an uncommon experience for Quincy, to have somebody place their reliance upon him in that way, and he was touched.

'How're you doin'?' Quincy asked, but one look at the man told him that the question was unnecessary. Birrell was failing fast. He wrapped the blanket carefully round the dying man's shoulders, taking great care not to brush against the arrow. Truth to tell though, it might have been a mercy to the injured man if the process of dying were to be speeded up a little. Birrell's face was grey and he was obviously in pain. Quincy thought that he probably didn't have the strength to speak again and was surprised when Birrell announced: 'Guess I won't ever open that detective agency after all, huh?'

'Ah, you never know,' Quincy replied in a joshing tone, 'I'll bet you been in tighter situations than this and still bounced back.' Then he looked at Birrell's face and knew that the end was near. This was no time for joking or false assurances. He said, 'You want me to say a prayer with you or something?'

Birrell's lips twitched slightly and he said, 'I reckon not. It looks awfully like hypocrisy at this late stage.' Then he closed his eyes and his breathing became more rapid and he began to shiver violently. Quincy was aware that the boy was standing beside him and he tried to spare him such a dreadful sight, by saying, 'Go walk on a bit over yonder, Bobby. This ain't a fittin' sight for you to see.'

'I want to stay with you, sir, if that's all right.'

'Come here,' said Quincy and drew the child to him. At that moment, Birrell took a great gulp of air into his lungs, shivered convulsively and then breathed out and was still. Quincy reached out and closed the dead man's eyes.

CHAPTER 12

When he was sure that Birrell was dead, Quincy stood up and said to Bobby, 'He was a right good man, a man you could trust. It's a shame he's dead.'

'What will happen now, Mr Quincy?' said the boy anxiously. 'What will become of us?'

'Why, the same as before, I reckon. Nothing's changed with our plans. We'll take this wagon.' Here Quincy paused to kick the nearest wheel. 'We'll take it on to Maricopa Wells.'

'What about him?' said Bobby, indicating with a trembling hand, the dead man.

'I don't like to do it, son, but we must leave the dead to bury the dead, like it says in the Good Book. We surely can't waste any time getting him under the ground, and I sure as . . . sure as the Lord made little apples, am not carrying a corpse along with us in the wagon. Come on, let's get moving.'

As gently as he could, Quincy dragged Birrell's

body clear of the wagon's wheels and laid it on its back. He wished that he could afford the dead man a decent burial, but his only concern now was to get that child to safety. There was nothing to be done, though, so he switched around the horses, harnessed one up to the wagon and tethered the other to the back. In that way, they set off east again.

The two of them made camp that night a little off the road. Bobby refused to move more than a foot or two from Quincy, seeing him as his only protection against a dangerous and uncertain world. And the good Lord alone knows, thought Quincy to himself, what is to become of this poor child when we hit Maricopa Wells. Still, that's not really my affair. It will be enough if I can do something for that Geoffrey Hanigan.

He still hadn't given any real thought as to how a wandering ragamuffin like him would be able to bestow over $3,000 in gold on a young boy. Quincy had always been a man who believed in taking one step at a time. He used sometimes to say to folk, 'That's why the Lord gives us just two legs, so we can only take one step at a time.'

Bobby himself touched upon his fate, when they had eaten and Quincy was brewing up a pot of coffee. He said, 'What will happen? When we get to town, I mean.'

'I'll level with you, son. I have not the faintest notion. You know anybody at all in Maricopa Wells?'

The boy shook his head. 'We didn't have a whole

lot to do with other folks. And I never knew any kin, 'cept for my ma and pa.'

'Well then, it's a puzzle for both of us, I guess.'

'You won't leave me, will you, sir? Not 'til something's decided?'

'I promise you that I won't. I'll take good care of you until I can find out what's to do.'

They reached Maricopa Wells about three the following day. Quincy wondered if he should make some report to the sheriff's office about the death of Birrell, but figuring that it would invite more questions than he felt able to answer, he shelved that proposal for the foreseeable future. After all, the sheriff wouldn't be able to restore the man to life, and there was no point in actively seeking out trouble.

When he booked them into a hotel, Quincy at first wanted to have separate rooms for the two of them. Bobby wasn't happy about being alone in a room, though, and begged him to try and arrange that they could both share a room. Quincy said to the clerk, 'Would it be possible for us to have a room with two beds?'

'Why yes, of course, sir,' replied the fellow, 'You and your son can share, that's no problem.'

It seemed easier and less likely to raise eyebrows if Quincy accepted this supposed relationship with the boy and as they headed to the stairs, he said to Bobby, winking at him, 'Come on . . . son.' The boy smiled at that, which gave Quincy a warm feeling in his heart.

After making provisions for the wagon and horses and stowing their things in the hotel, Quincy took the boy to a nearby eating house for a proper, cooked meal. Various newspapers were provided for the patrons to read, while waiting for their orders and one of these was the latest copy of the *Tucson Weekly Intelligencer and Agricultural Gazette*. Quincy scanned it with interest. There, on the front page, was an article which concerned him very closely. It read:

Astonishing and Heartwarming
Outcome for Orphaned Boy

Readers of this publication will recall the tragic circumstances which robbed young widow **ESTHER HANIGAN** of her life a short while back. Her killers remain at liberty, while there was every chance that her only child, **GEOFFEY HANIGAN**, would be forced into the Tucson Orphans' Asylum; his nearest relative and the woman who had taken him in, being all but destitute herself. How shall we tell readers of the generosity of the Southern Pacific Railroad Company, who announced yesterday that they are to make an *ex gratia* payment to **GEOFFREY HANIGAN**'s aunt of the sum of $2,000? Nor is this all. Moved by the plight of this poor child, readers of the *Tucson Weekly Intelligencer and Agricultural Gazette* have been sending money in to this newspaper to be

forwarded to the family of young **GEOFFREY**.
To date, this money totals an amazing $1,518!
The proprietors of the *Tucson Weekly*
Intelligencer and Agricultural Gazette have gener-
ously contributed another $500, so **GEOFFREY**
HANIGAN is no longer destined for an
orphanage. He and his aunt desire it to be
known how grateful they are for this bounty
and wish to thank all those readers of this
newspaper who were moved to dip into their
pockets in this way.

'Well, that's a good bit of publicity for the railroad
company,' muttered Quincy, 'And for the paper
too.'

'What's that, sir?' asked Bobby.

'Nothing at all, son. Just talking to myself is all.'
It seemed to Quincy that with $4,000 or so provided
for him, perhaps he would not after all have to
devise some complicated plan for bestowing his
share of the proceeds of the robbery on the boy
and his aunt. This was a relief indeed, for he had
not yet come up with even a tentative scheme for
handing over a load of stolen gold to a complete
stranger.

The meal was most welcome and a distinct
improvement on the partly broiled and mostly raw
food upon which Quincy and the boy had for the last
few days been subsisting. Quincy watched Bobby rav-
enously devouring a chicken leg. He said, 'There's
plenty more in the kitchen, son. You don't need to

gnaw the bones.'

After they had eaten their fill, Quincy said, 'Are you telling me, Bobby, that there is not one relative that you have ever met or heard of? Not one?'

'That's about it, Mr Quincy. We kept ourselves to ourselves and moved about from time to time. I never even heard tell of any other family.'

Quincy thought the matter over and then said, 'I'm goin' to lay down my cards, Bobby, and you can make of them what you will. I have enough cash money to buy a little place. By which I mean a small farm or some such. I doubt I'll have enough to buy some fancy house to go with it, but I've built a soddy before. You know what that is?'

'Yes, sir,' said Bobby, his eyes lighting up with interest. 'That's just what Pa said we would live in when we got to our quarter section. He said as we'd have to plough up some prairie and then build a house from the turfs. Isn't that what you're talkin' of?'

'Yes, that's about right. Here's the point that I'm coming to. I ain't about to abandon you, so you can rest easy on that score. We got us two choices. You know what they are?'

'No, I don't know at all, Mr Quincy,' said the child, looking immensely woe-begone, 'But I guess as you're tellin' me here's where we part.'

'That's up to you. Here's how things stand. We can go now to the sheriff's office and I can tell him the whole, entire story of how we chanced to meet and then he can arrange for you to stay with some kind person who will look after you 'til enquiries can be made and some kin o' yours tracked down.'

Bobby's expression said clearly that he was not too taken with this first option. He said, 'What'll happen if we don't do that, sir?'

'Well then, here's the only other way I can see us proceeding and that's with you and me staying together and you comin' to live with me on this farm I mean to start. Mind, it'll be hard work for the both of us if we take that road, and there's no denying it.'

The words were no sooner out of Quincy's mouth than the boy got up from his chair, came round the table and threw his arms around the astonished man.

'Do you really mean it, sir? Honestly and truly?'

'Wouldn't have said it, if'n I didn't mean it,' said Quincy gruffly, although he was secretly pleased at the boy's reception of his proposal. 'Mind, though, what I tell you, this isn't apt to be a vacation, nor anything like it, you hear what I'm telling you?'

'Yes, sir, I heard.'

'Anyways, we'd best be seeing about you getting to bed now. You look like you could do with a proper night's sleep in a real bed.' Bobby made no protest about this and allowed himself to be guided back to the hotel and settled beneath the sheets of his cot.

'You won't . . . you won't leave me, will you, Mr Quincy?'

'What, while you're sleeping? No. 'Less I need to

158

go downstairs for a minute. I won't leave the hotel, don't you fret about that.'

In no time at all, the child's eyes were closed and he was fast asleep. Quincy adjusted the bedclothes around the boy and then went over to the window. The sun had dipped below the horizon and it would soon be dark. Over across town, he could see smoke rising from the railroad depot; he supposed that a train must have arrived. In the morning, he would have to see about buying some land, but he had no real apprehension about that. The current economic climate was such that farmers were going bust every day of the week, and he didn't anticipate too much trouble in running to earth one of those failed men who would jump at the chance of getting two or two and a half thousand dollars for their land.

There was a mournful whistle in the distance as the train prepared to depart. Quincy had never had much to do with children before and felt a certain degree of trepidation about the idea of sharing his life with one at this age. Still and all though, men managed to do that all the time and what one man could do, Quincy reckoned that he could too. He had had it in mind to go down to the bar and have a glass of whiskey before retiring, but the more he thought about it, the more tired he felt. He thought that he'd just turn in himself and go to sleep right this minute. He went over to check on the boy and, on a sudden impulse, he stooped down and kissed the child's forehead. Then he prepared for bed and climbed beneath the sheets of the other bed. He fell asleep almost as quickly as Bobby had done.